A. M. JENKINS

DAMAGE

HARPERCOLLINS*PUBLISHERS*

Thanks to Jeff Jenkins for sharing his knowledge of football (any errors or exaggerations regarding that sport lie solely at the feet of the author) and to Rachel Safko for her help in preparing this manuscript. Also, many thanks to the members of the Four Star Coffee Bar critique group and the YAWRITER list, for putting up with my writerly angst; I'm especially grateful to Cathy Atkins, Lisa Firke, Adrianne Fitzpatrick, Judy Gregerson, Shirley Harazin, Denise Johns, Kathy Lay, Ann Manheimer, Melissa Russell, Andrea Schulz, Shelley Sykes, Melissa Wyatt, and Lidia Zenida, and would like to thank them for their insights. I owe a tremendous debt to Martha Moore, Jan Peck, and Laura Wiess, for opening their hearts and helping me to write as honestly and deeply as I could. And finally, this book would not be here without Steve Malk, who took an enormous burden from my shoulders and offered to carry it for me, and Alix Reid, who believed in and cared for Austin from the moment she met him.

Library of Congress Cataloging-in-Publication Data

Jenkins, A. M. (Amanda McRaney)

Damage / by Amanda Jenkins.

p.   cm.

Summary: Seventeen-year-old football hero Austin, trying to understand the inexplicable depression that has drained his interest in life, thinks he has found relief in a girl who seems very special.

ISBN 0-06-029099-4 — ISBN 0-06-029100-1 (lib. bdg.)

[1. Depression, Mental—Fiction. 2. Football—Fiction.] I. Title.

PZ7.J4125 Dam 2001   00-054038

[Fic]—dc21   CIP

                                                                                               AC

Typography by Alison Donalty

7   9   10   8   6

❖

First Edition

For those who are struggling; for those who have made it through; for those who have been left behind

CHAPTER ONE

It's all yours. Your hands rise, fingers spread, ready to feel the firm scrape of the football, ready to pull it to you, ready to tuck it safely in.

But the ball bumbles against your fingertips. It lurches away, and that beautiful spiraling pass ends its life in a series of ugly bounces across the field.

Then there's just a football lying untended on the grass, just that—and your empty hands.

When you open your eyes, the joyless feeling has already crawled onto your chest. The ceiling of your room presses you down into the mattress. The air settles in your lungs so heavy that it's almost too much trouble to breathe.

You kind of remember having some bad dreams, but you can't remember what they were. You just lie there, flat as the faded streak of afternoon sunlight that slants through the western window and impales your bed.

It's almost night. You're supposed to pick up Curtis and Dobie, so the three of you can go out. Your eyes move, skimming the room, trying to grab hold of anything that will break the suction of the bed.

A newspaper clipping tacked to the bulletin board. It's a black-and-white head shot of a guy in a football jersey, and underneath in bold print:

AUSTIN REID: PRIDE OF THE PARKERSVILLE PANTHERS

That picture smiled out of the sports section during last year's state semifinals. Now it smiles out over the bedroom.

It's you.

Shoot, that guy in the picture there wouldn't lie around on a Saturday night. He wouldn't think how it's too much trouble to *breathe*.

So you roll slowly to sit up. Get to your feet. Lumber down the hall, past your sister Becky's room, into the bathroom. Stop in front of the sink. Raise your head to look into the mirror.

The guy reflected back at you is the same one from the picture. Only he's not smiling. And he hasn't got a jersey on. Not even a shirt. But still, that *is* him—dark hair, straight white teeth, a strong jawline, a nose that's not anything special.

You lean forward, looking into his eyes. They're blue.

What do other people see when they look into them—those eyes in the mirror? Are they flat? Cold?

Or just nothing at all?

You look harder, trying to feel anything for him. You try to get him to smile, to see if that will help.

All you can get is a dull stare.

Your gaze slides down to your own hands. Even now they can almost feel the football bulleting into them. Your hands are big, strong. Like your dad's hands, you remember, even though he died when you were only three. That's what you remember about him; strong hands, lifting you up to sit on the bathroom counter.

You're staring at your hands and the memory runs, like a movie: the hiss of shaving cream escaping into a frothy white pile; the sharp clean scent. The soft light foam hanging off your cheeks like a floppy beard. The connection, you and your dad, both scraping tracks in white lather, you with a toy razor.

You raise your head to stare into the mirror again. Those three-year-old cheeks belonged to you. Not some guy in a picture. You.

You turn the faucet handle all the way to the right. Shoot, there's plenty of people who are abused or neglected, plenty of people who would probably love to have your particular life instead of their own. Your life that's a gift from God.

3

It'll be an outright sin if you don't snap out of feeling this way.

The water rushes down the drain, running from cold to hot, sounding so alive and urgent that it gives you the traction you need to climb out of this rut.

Okay. So you're going to clean up a little. Then you're going to put on a fresh shirt. Put on that smile, like clicking on a button.

And then you're going to go out.

You've parked your truck in the usual spot, past your country neighborhood with its patchwork of trailers, houses, small farms, and ranch land, out where the old railroad tracks disappear into dirt and tall grass. You and Curtis are sitting on the tailgate, but Dobie slouches long legged in the bed of the pickup, carelessly leaning against the wheel well next to the ice chest.

This is partying, Parkersville style.

Your beer bottle's empty now, but you don't move to throw it away.

"You all right?" Curtis asks, eyeing you as he takes another swig from his longneck. Curtis Hightower is your closest friend, your next-door neighbor, too—not in the town sense, where neighbors live right in one another's back pockets without ever knowing each other, but in the country sense, where neighbors are like family, yet everybody's got a little elbow room.

2

Sure enough, the first week of practice is like sliding into a well-worn groove. There's no doubt you'll be starting. Your body, at least, still seems to have a fierce interest in the details and mechanics of football. Inside you still feel pretty much like a flattened tire, but it's not too hard to shove that feeling down and just keep putting one foot in front of the other.

This is Coach Van Zandt's first year at Parkersville. Nobody knows yet how far he can be pushed. All anybody knows is that he used to be in the marines, and he's passionate about his job.

After one play, when everybody's heading back to the line, Coach gives his baseball cap a furious tug. "Stargill!" he bellows. "Whatcha doing lying in the dirt?"

Brett Stargill lumbers to his feet, towering over Coach. Coach's paunchy stomach is the only part of him

"Yeah," you say. You *are* all right, and what would you tell him, anyway? *Sometimes I can't face getting out of bed? Sometimes I feel so crushed I can't move?* Like Curtis can do anything about it anyway. "I'm fine," you add.

Dobie pats the ice chest. "Want another?"

"No thanks."

Dobie looks at you for a moment, confused like a dog, like you didn't speak his particular brand of English. Then he nods. "It won't hurt to lay off for one night," he says, as if to comfort you. "You drank enough at the lake last week to last you through a dry spell."

"Hell, Austy's probably still getting over that one." Curtis swings his legs idly, as relaxed looking as ever, but his dark eyes are sharp on you. He does that sometimes, his words dry and teasing, his eyes searching.

Tonight you think they might be searching for something Curtis feels but can't name. You swing your legs, too, your hands gripping the edge of the tailgate, trying to think of the right words to say. Curtis has a head-on, outspoken way of looking at things, and you don't particularly want him looking at you right now.

Click. You grin. "I think it's a good idea to leave some of the drinking to the other guys," the Pride of the Panthers announces in just the right voice. "That way they'll all be busy burping and pissing while I'm out chasing the ladies."

Curtis chuckles. You relax.

"They ain't ladies once you get through with them, Austin," Dobie remarks.

"Now, why do you say that?" you ask, to egg him on. Curtis just listens, his eyes roaming out into the darkness now. "Why shouldn't they have a good time, too, without you calling them sluts?"

"I didn't call nobody a slut."

"Are you saying you'd marry some girl who's slept around?"

"Well, no, but that's different."

"Nobody's going to marry Dobie," Curtis says, deadpan. "Not with that beer gut he's getting."

"So are you," Dobie shoots back. Dobie believes anything anybody says to him. Curtis is exaggerating about his beer gut; in fact he is outright lying. Dobie is tall and thin and mostly cowboy hat and legs and belt buckle. He isn't muscular like you or even wiry like Curtis. He's just Dobie.

Curtis laughs and takes another drink. Curtis has a cowboy hat, but he doesn't wear it much, and he doesn't have a beer gut, either. He isn't the type to argue if he knows he's right.

You set the empty bottle down beside you. Girls are another thing that's not right anymore. The Pride of the Panthers has always had a girlfriend—but you haven't had one in a while. Just haven't been able to get interested. The way you haven't been able to get interested in much of anything.

That joyless feeling is out there in the around the pickup, hanging like a low cloud; y its edges brush against you.

Curtis drains the last of his beer and tosses into the bushes. He hasn't dated anybody Hopkins broke up with him in the spring, and want to talk about girls, either.

"Two-a-days start Monday," you say to particular, and saying it almost makes you f better. Not that you're looking forward to through sprints and conditioning drills, lin sweltering pads. But Monday morning you v the option of wallowing around in bed like yo summer; you'll be out there in the late August what you're told.

You've always played for sheer fun. P games, doesn't matter which—there's nothing ning the play and actually having it work, turr the ball coming at you, feeling it fly straight hands as if it's been sucked there.

On Monday, you're pretty sure, you'll wak the sun, and find that this drag-down feeling away like some bad dream.

as wide as Brett. Still, Brett just shrugs, eyes on the ground.

"You ain't hurt 'less I say you're hurt."

Curtis said earlier in the week that Coach thinks he's some kind of drill sergeant. He said that's okay, though, since Coach takes his football seriously. Curtis takes his football seriously, too.

When Coach hollers, "Water break!" nobody needs to be told twice to take off for the coolers Dobie has set up on the bottom row of the bleachers.

You get in line with Curtis, waiting for the water cooler on the end. Both of you are a little apart from all the jostling and joking. Both of your gray practice jerseys are dark with sweat. Curtis holds his helmet under one arm. His hair is sweat-plastered to his head.

You undo your chin strap but don't take off your helmet. Instead, you just stand there, staring out at a world framed by rigid plastic edges.

"You've been playing different," Curtis says out of the blue. "You're not as focused as you usually are."

Now you see that his dark eyes are on you; they've got that sharp, considering look. If he thinks you're going to spill your guts, he's wrong. There aren't any words for what you feel sometimes, and, anyway, there's nothing to talk about.

The guy in front of Curtis steps away from the cooler, but Curtis hasn't noticed. "You're the one needs to pay attention," you say, and give him a friendly shove toward the cooler.

Curtis picks up and fills a paper cup, and everything moves one step closer to normal. While he drains the cup in one long swallow, you pull the silence around you like a blanket. He bends to fill the cup a second time, dumps the whole thing over his head, and shakes like a dog, sending drops of water flying.

Now it's your turn. You push your helmet up and gulp down aching cold water, letting some run down your chin and neck to cool your front.

Everybody else is straggling onto the field. You crumple the cup, toss it into the trash, and turn to walk back, too.

"Hey," Curtis says, not moving. "Austy."

His tone stops you in your tracks. You turn to look at him. Curtis's eyes are brown, but not the soft brown most people have. They can be hard like a flint striking sparks, if he's angry. Which isn't often; Curtis doesn't let much get to him. Right now, though, his eyes are zeroed in on you with the intensity that means there's some kind of emotion backed up behind them.

"It's not just football," he says. "You've been acting different. Out of it. Like you just woke up. Or like you're some old man, in slow motion. Hey. You know you can talk to me, don't you? If anything's wrong?"

Curtis is quiet, not much of a talker. But he's one hell of an observer.

"Yeah," you say. You *are* all right, and what would you tell him, anyway? *Sometimes I can't face getting out of bed? Sometimes I feel so crushed I can't move?* Like Curtis can do anything about it anyway. "I'm fine," you add.

Dobie pats the ice chest. "Want another?"

"No thanks."

Dobie looks at you for a moment, confused like a dog, like you didn't speak his particular brand of English. Then he nods. "It won't hurt to lay off for one night," he says, as if to comfort you. "You drank enough at the lake last week to last you through a dry spell."

"Hell, Austy's probably still getting over that one." Curtis swings his legs idly, as relaxed looking as ever, but his dark eyes are sharp on you. He does that sometimes, his words dry and teasing, his eyes searching.

Tonight you think they might be searching for something Curtis feels but can't name. You swing your legs, too, your hands gripping the edge of the tailgate, trying to think of the right words to say. Curtis has a head-on, outspoken way of looking at things, and you don't particularly want him looking at you right now.

Click. You grin. "I think it's a good idea to leave some of the drinking to the other guys," the Pride of the Panthers announces in just the right voice. "That way they'll all be busy burping and pissing while I'm out chasing the ladies."

Curtis chuckles. You relax.

5

"They ain't ladies once you get through with them, Austin," Dobie remarks.

"Now, why do you say that?" you ask, to egg him on. Curtis just listens, his eyes roaming out into the darkness now. "Why shouldn't they have a good time, too, without you calling them sluts?"

"I didn't call nobody a slut."

"Are you saying you'd marry some girl who's slept around?"

"Well, no, but that's different."

"Nobody's going to marry Dobie," Curtis says, deadpan. "Not with that beer gut he's getting."

"So are you," Dobie shoots back. Dobie believes anything anybody says to him. Curtis is exaggerating about his beer gut; in fact he is outright lying. Dobie is tall and thin and mostly cowboy hat and legs and belt buckle. He isn't muscular like you or even wiry like Curtis. He's just Dobie.

Curtis laughs and takes another drink. Curtis has a cowboy hat, but he doesn't wear it much, and he doesn't have a beer gut, either. He isn't the type to argue if he knows he's right.

You set the empty bottle down beside you. Girls are another thing that's not right anymore. The Pride of the Panthers has always had a girlfriend—but you haven't had one in a while. Just haven't been able to get interested. The way you haven't been able to get interested in much of anything.

That joyless feeling is out there in the darkness round the pickup, hanging like a low cloud; you can feel its edges brush against you.

Curtis drains the last of his beer and tosses the bottle into the bushes. He hasn't dated anybody since Kat Hopkins broke up with him in the spring, and he doesn't want to talk about girls, either.

"Two-a-days start Monday," you say to nobody in particular, and saying it almost makes you feel a little better. Not that you're looking forward to sweating through sprints and conditioning drills, line drills in sweltering pads. But Monday morning you won't have the option of wallowing around in bed like you have all summer; you'll be out there in the late August sun doing what you're told.

You've always played for sheer fun. Practice or games, doesn't matter which—there's nothing like running the play and actually having it work, turning to see the ball coming at you, feeling it fly straight into your hands as if it's been sucked there.

On Monday, you're pretty sure, you'll wake up with the sun, and find that this drag-down feeling has faded away like some bad dream.

2

Sure enough, the first week of practice is like sliding into a well-worn groove. There's no doubt you'll be starting. Your body, at least, still seems to have a fierce interest in the details and mechanics of football. Inside you still feel pretty much like a flattened tire, but it's not too hard to shove that feeling down and just keep putting one foot in front of the other.

This is Coach Van Zandt's first year at Parkersville. Nobody knows yet how far he can be pushed. All anybody knows is that he used to be in the marines, and he's passionate about his job.

After one play, when everybody's heading back to the line, Coach gives his baseball cap a furious tug. "Stargill!" he bellows. "Whatcha doing lying in the dirt?"

Brett Stargill lumbers to his feet, towering over Coach. Coach's paunchy stomach is the only part of him

"Nothing's wrong," you tell him. It's true. It *is*—because you've got nothing to complain about. Nothing to explain, nothing that makes any sense. Nothing that's a *real* problem, like what other people have.

Take Curtis. It was about five years ago you found him in the tack room out by your family's barn. He was sitting with his back to the wall, knees drawn up, head buried on his arms, so he didn't know you were there. You could tell he was crying, and you turned to sneak away—but that didn't seem right, so you came back and sat down beside him without saying anything, and just kind of kept him company till he was finished. You didn't look at him or ask about it, and he never did say what happened—but you had an idea what it was about. Sure enough, right after that his father left for Nevada with one of the summer interns from his law office.

Curtis never did talk about it much, but he spent quite a bit of time that fall out in the wooded acres behind your house, sawing up an old dead tree and hauling the chunks to your family's barn to chop them small before flinging them onto the woodpile. Hardly said a word about his dad—but for a long time after that, whenever you went over to the Hightowers', you felt like there was an invisible hole right in the heart of the house; a jagged hole that everybody walked around and nobody talked about. It's still there, even five years later—though now it's not so huge and the edges have smoothed.

But in your life, there are no holes. Your house is just

a house like anybody else's. And you've got nothing to talk about.

"I've just been a little tired," you tell Curtis.

"Reid and Hightower!" Coach is hollering. "Get your asses in gear! Time to get back to work!"

The two of you start running back.

"Cox! Try to get the goddamn ball in the *air* this time."

As everybody lines up you can see Curtis's eyes on you. Impersonal now; you're just an object he has to track and follow.

"Blue thirty-four!" Cox shouts. "Blue thirty-four! Set . . . Hut! Hut!"

You sprint forward and cut inside. You can feel Curtis shadowing you, but the ball is spiraling toward you. You stretch out your hands, ready to feel the clean smack of the catch.

It doesn't come. Curtis gets a hand up; the two of you get tangled up somehow and you both come down in a heap on the grass.

Curtis gets immediately to his feet; he's in his usual between plays half awareness and barely gives you a glance as he scoops up the ball and tosses it back to the center.

You lie outstretched on the turf and wait for your breath to come back into your lungs.

"Reid!" Coach hollers. "You don't jump up and get

moving, you better be able to show me some bone sticking out!"

So you get up, panting; Curtis has already trotted back to the line.

You follow. Alone and empty-handed.

After practice on Friday, Curtis asks if you and Dobie want to go grab a burger or something.

"Sure," you answer, although you're not really hungry. There's nothing else to do, and, besides, there'll be plenty of people down at the Dairy Queen. It's easier to click on that button around a lot of people. Easier to go through the motions of having a good time.

You drive, Curtis rides shotgun, Dobie's in the back. The pickup bumps across the field house parking lot, bottles rattling and bouncing around in the bed.

Since it's Friday night, the Dairy Queen is pretty crowded. You have to park way back in the corner of the lot, next to the close-cropped grass lawn of the church next door. When you get out of the truck, you're close enough to read the weekly quote-on-a-sign in front.

First Baptist Church of Parkersville, Texas

BE JOYFUL ALWAYS.

1 Thess 5:16

Curtis gets out and slams the door. Dobie climbs over the tailgate. You stand there looking at that sign—the three little words in bold black letters: *Be joyful always.* It's almost like God's speaking to you personally.

Things are about to get under control. Sure they are. Once the season starts, they will. Every year since ninth grade, crossing that goal line for the first time pumps you so full of joy, it all overflows and gets reflected back by a thousand people in the stands feeling the same thing. That first Friday night always puffs you up so light you could float out of the stadium and onto the bus.

This is senior year. It's bound to be great.

It's going to be a great year.

You join Curtis and Dobie, walking across the parking lot. "I'm kind of hungry, too," Dobie's saying. "I might have a burger or two just to keep y'all company. Oh, man," he adds. "Look who's here."

He nods toward the cherry red Miata parked in front, a bright patch of color between the fluorescent lights and the darkness.

And there they are next to it—Heather Mackenzie and Melissa Larkin, standing at an outside table, talking to some other girls. You dated Melissa for a while last year; it was an amicable breakup and the two of you still get along fine. And Heather is hands down the most beautiful girl in town, the number one girl on every guy's "Top Ten To Do" list.

But that's not the only reason she captures your eye. It's because you've always thought she's like a jigsaw puzzle that's just a little bit incomplete. And you like the feeling of holding someone else's missing piece in your hand.

"Look at Austin, making plans," Dobie observes. "You can just about see the gears turning."

You weren't really making any plans at all, but now you have to make a big point of looking like you were. So you walk a little slower and let a slow-moving grin take over your whole face while your eyes take a little extra time appreciating Heather's long legs.

"Aw, I was just kidding," Dobie says quickly. "You know she won't go out with nobody our age. Remember how she shot Cox down when he asked her out in front of everybody?"

Yeah, you heard about that. But still you look at Heather—there's something like a string pulling your eyes toward her. Heather's like you; her father died when she was little. Of course, nobody talks about it, not right out. When Heather moved here in the third grade, the story was that her parents were divorced, and her dad was still in Ohio. But somehow word leaked out that Mr. Mackenzie killed himself, and, of course, the news zipped along phone lines and flashed in whispers from ear to ear. It's been years since you've heard anybody mention it—but that hasn't kept you from thinking about it, from wondering whether the Mackenzie house has a dark jagged hole at the heart of it, like Curtis's, or whether it's just a house, like yours.

Tonight the first thing that captures your eyes, like always, is Heather's rear end, tight and tilted like the back of a Camaro; and when that brief surge of interest is gone you look a little longer anyway, wondering if she's ever had to click on a button or two to get Heather Mackenzie up and running.

Curtis doesn't slow, just walks right past them; the only thing he's interested in is that Kat's not at any of these outside tables. You don't say anything to Dobie, and you certainly don't say anything to Heather. You just follow Curtis through the door.

Inside at the counter, he stands beside you scanning the room the way he always does since he and Kat went their separate ways.

"Parkersville's got five thousand people in it, right?" Curtis's eyes flick from booth to booth.

"Uh-huh."

"So how come we keep seeing the same ones over and over?"

"Beats me," you say, knowing what Curtis really means is the ones he keeps seeing don't include Katherine Hopkins. Curtis can be pretty negative sometimes. He wouldn't hesitate a moment to sit there like a lump in the middle of everybody else's good time. On the other hand, there's you; if God sends you a personal message to be joyful always, you're going to take it seriously.

So when one of your little sister's friends walks by, you reach out and give her ponytail a gentle tug. She's been at your house a couple of times, but you can't remember her name. She whirls around, breaks into a big smile, and says "Hi, Austin." Exactly the kind of light friendly contact that helps pin things together so that the bottom doesn't drop out of the evening.

When the food's ready you get down to the business at hand: eating. This hamburger is the first meal you've had today, and you may not be hungry, but your body's going to wolf down every bite.

"God, Austin, don't they feed you at home?" Becky's friend calls boldly from a nearby booth. She's little, freshman-sized, underdeveloped—and she's got on enough makeup to pave Highway 171.

Her tablemates are giggling. "I must have missed a meal," you tell her, flashing a grin that dissolves the giggles into elbow poking. "Either that, or I'm having a growth spurt."

Dobie has just taken a bite, but at the words "growth spurt," he starts snickering into his hamburger.

"Now, Dobie," you tell him, "get your mind out of the gutter. There's nothing dirty about a little *spurt* now and then." Normally, calling attention to Dobie in front of females would make him slide under the table—but

17

right now all he can do is set the hamburger down and put his hands over his face, and try to stop laughing long enough to swallow.

Curtis eyes Dobie. "You're not choking, are you?"

Dobie shakes his head frantically, behind his hands. His ears are beet red.

"Maybe you ought to whack him on the back a couple times, Austy," Curtis suggests.

Dobie shakes his head again. After a few more moments he manages to swallow, and lowers his hands. "Don't do that, man. Don't make me laugh while I'm eating." His face is getting back to its normal color.

"All I said was I'm having a growth spurt." You start to add something about spurts being against the penal code—"penal code" being a surefire Dobie cracker-upper ever since eighth-grade social studies.

But Dobie's attention has been caught by something outside the window. "Dang," he mutters. "I think I'm getting a growth spurt right now."

You turn to look. It's Heather again, still outside. This time she's bending forward to lean over the table. It is amazing, the lines a plain old pair of jeans can take on when a girl is wearing them. You feel like a dog perking up its ears.

Curtis has long since given up looking around for Kat. He's just stirring a straw around and around in the cup he hasn't taken a drink from. If Curtis was a dog right now, his ears would be limp and drooping.

You notice that Heather has one thumb hooked through a belt loop; the other hand flips her hair back over her shoulder. It crosses your mind that she knows how good she looks in those jeans, and wants everybody else to know, too.

Well, they do.

The light dusts her hair so that it looks almost golden. She looks a lot like one of those Barbie dolls Becky used to play with a few years ago—only nobody could ever make a doll so alive and perfect.

Heather turns her head and sees you through the window.

She gives you a smile so big and so bright that it lifts the breath up out of your chest. Somehow it doesn't seem to be directed at Curtis or Dobie, although they're sitting right next to you.

You nod hello back, then turn to Curtis, though you're still watching her out of the corner of your eye.

"So," you ask Curtis, "what do you think?"

"'Bout what?"

"About Heather." You figure you already know, but you're in the habit of prodding Curtis out of his Kat-based bad moods.

Curtis doesn't even bother to look out the window. "I think she's shallow and manipulates people," he says, and starts fooling around with Dairy Queen physics; holding one finger over the end of his straw, lifting it, letting the air pressure keep the Coke in the straw.

Curtis is usually right about people. Curtis can peel people like onions.

But Heather's looking at you right now, and she says something to her friends out of the side of her mouth, so that the whole circle of girls collapses in a flurry of giggles and glances cast your way.

And you're supposed to play along with this game. You've always played it well; flirting, dating, getting laid—all without leaving a trail of hurt feelings behind—have always been Austin Reid's home territory.

Now Heather turns away; she's talking with her friends, flashing that beauty queen smile like she was just crowned Miss Texas.

Watching Heather, you wonder if she ever feels like the glue holding that smile to her face is slowly disintegrating.

CHAPTER THREE

The alarm clock has been going off for a while. It rasps the air, nagging, insistent.

Today is the first day of school.

You manage to pull the pillow away but can't get the energy to sit up. Through bleary eyes you see the alarm on the nightstand and reach out, clamp down on it till it shuts up.

Okay. You know what you have to do. Don't even think—just get up. Just get on your feet and start moving—don't stop to sit on the edge of the bed, don't wait for your head to clear, don't pause at all. Just roll out of bed and keep going.

You feel that guy in the picture, that Pride of the Panthers, looking at you, greeting you from his newspaper clipping. When your eyes grab hold of him he's grinning that blank grin; he's one pushpin away from being blank cork staring out from a flat wall, but he still seems more real than you are.

So you do what you're supposed to; get out of bed, walk down the hall into the bathroom, shut the door, and turn on the faucet.

While waiting for the water to run hot, you take the wooden box off its shelf in the medicine cabinet and feel the heft of that golden razor in your hand. You almost feel like your dad's with you right now, admiring the smooth curve of the handle, the sharp glint of the blade's edge.

Shave, shower, get dressed.

When you walk into the kitchen Mom is still there, bustling around the kitchen. Usually she's gone by this time, but right now she's hurriedly packing her lunch. "Austin," she says, "could you reach in the fridge and get me that baggie of carrot sticks?"

It's on the top shelf behind the milk. You hand Mom her carrot sticks and then get the milk out, too, because that's all you have for breakfast anymore.

"Thanks." Mom stuffs the baggie into a brown paper sack. She's got a run down the back of one stocking, but she looks pretty harried, and you can't decide whether you should mention it. "Now, where are those crackers?" she mutters to herself.

"Right there on the counter." You pour your milk into a glass. If she weren't here you'd just drink it from the carton.

"Oh. Thanks. Hey, how about if you put some of those muscles to work and open the mayonnaise for me?"

There's a jar on the counter. You pick it up, grip the jar lid, and give it a twist. No luck.

Mom's got her back to you; the paper sack crackles as she dumps the crackers in. "You look a little tired," she says, without turning around. "Feeling okay?"

How does she do that? She hasn't even looked at you this morning.

You frown down at the stubborn lid. You could tell her about not sleeping well, but you don't often talk to her about stuff, how you feel about things. Not because she's mean or won't listen. It's just that you're a seventeen-year-old senior football player, and she's a forty-year-old office administrator who's been working overtime for almost two years now, and your lives don't overlap much.

"Mo-o-om?" Becky calls from down the hall.

"In here," Mom hollers, and glances at the clock. You give the lid another straining twist and it comes free. "Thanks." She takes the jar from your hand and turns back to the counter as Becky comes in, wearing one of her new pairs of jeans. Becky spent the largest portion of her school clothes money on two pairs of jeans, because she would rather wear the "right" clothes than have ten on-sale pairs of pants. No matter that now she's got to do laundry every night to have something clean to wear the next day. The only thing that matters to Becky is that she wears exactly what her friends wear.

"I'm begging you, Mother." The words may be begging, but Becky's mouth is pinched up for a fight. "Please, please, please let me wear my new blouse?"

Mom dips a butter knife into the mayonnaise and starts slapping mayo on bread. Her knife doesn't stop moving as she glances over at Becky, who's wearing some blue shirt that comes partway off her shoulders. "No. I told you to take that thing back to the store."

"Allie's got one just like this, and her parents don't care."

"That's why I don't want you going to Allie's house."

"It's just a summer top. It'll keep me cool—it's not like it's revealing or anything."

"You can't wear a bra under it. Go change."

"Mother—"

"No. Don't ask me again," Mom warns. She tosses the knife into the sink with a clatter.

Becky's eyebrows come together like thunderclouds. She looks the way she did when she was four, and you told her to quit following you and Curtis around. "I'm not a child anymore."

"Don't even start," Mom says, grimly laying turkey slices on bread.

"I was going to ask if I could go home with Allie today, but now I'm not because you're just going to say no. So I'll just say thanks, Mom—thanks for not trusting me and for ruining my life."

"Your life is just fine, miss." Mom drops the top piece of bread onto her sandwich and turns to Becky. Each glares at the other with the exact same bulldog stubbornness before Mom turns back to the counter to stuff her sandwich into a fresh baggie. "I refuse to lose my temper, because I'm already late." She drops the sandwich into her paper sack, crumples the top down. "Austin," she says briskly, "your sister interrupted. You're not coming down with anything, are you?"

She stops moving and waits for an answer. But her eyes are still angry, like they haven't quite let go of the argument with Becky. And her short dark hair is still damp, because she's late for work and didn't have time to dry it this morning. And there's still a run in her stocking that she doesn't know about.

You're not going to tell her. "I'm okay. I just woke up and couldn't get back to sleep, is all."

"Try to take a nap when you get home, okay?" Mom gives you a quick, tight smile, snatches her purse off the counter, and moves to the door. "Lock this behind me, will you? Becky, I'm going to call at four o'clock sharp. You better be here to answer the phone." Then she's out the door, her purse falling down off her shoulder.

The screen door bangs shut, the *Wild Horses* wall calendar next to the refrigerator flutters a little before settling back into place. Years ago, Mom tried to make a go of her own business of breaking and training horses, but there just wasn't enough money in it. That calendar, with its soft-focus photographs, is your mom's only acknowl-edgment that she ever had dreams of anything besides working in an office.

"Everybody gets to do everything they want, except for me." Becky is standing next to you, arms folded, face sulky. "Even you get to do what you want, just because you're a boy," she says, as if it's all your fault she has to go change her blouse. "Nobody cares what you wear." Her eyebrows are coming together again. "*And* you got all the eyelashes. *And* you hardly ever get a zit."

She whirls around and stomps down the hall, leaving you alone.

You can spend your time standing here like a zombie, or you can get moving, too.

Okay. Time to change the channel. You should drink what's left of your milk. Better get something down, since you won't have lunch till after noon.

But you really don't want it anymore, so you pour the rest of your breakfast down the kitchen sink.

Becky hurries by on her way to catch the bus. She's wearing a denim jacket and holding her books over her chest, so you have no idea if she's wearing the forbidden blouse. She unbends enough to mutter a "Bye," at you before she scuttles out the door.

"Bye," you tell her, even though the screen door has already slammed behind her, and you're alone again.

Okay. After twelve years of school, you can get into the routine, make all the right moves and say all the right words by habit. All the actions from all the years before have embedded themselves in your brain.

So you go brush your teeth, grab a couple bucks out of the jar for lunch, lock the back door on your way out.

Once in your truck it's down the highway, turn right into the parking lot, straight to the area by the field house where all the athletes park. Get there right as the bell's ringing. Go straight to homeroom, sit and mess around with your friends till you get your locker assignment. Head to that first class and sit while the teacher wrestles with the roll, with latecomers, with people in the wrong class, passes out a Xeroxed sheet of class rules and after everybody's read it, reads the whole thing out loud anyway. Then there's stacks of books waiting to be handed out, chalkboards full of words to be copied, more xeroxed sheets filled with more words that nobody wants to read—or hear.

The whole day is like trying to sing a song that's had all the music drained out.

At lunch it's the same as all the other years. The athletes eat together off campus at the Dairy Queen. The talk runs to practice, girls, classes.

It's hot as Hades at the outside tables in the Dairy Queen parking lot, so you and Curtis and Dobie and Brett eat inside. Through the window you can see the First Baptist Church hasn't gotten around to changing its sign yet. *Be joyful always.*

Dobie's only concern is food. You're forcing yourself

to eat; you take a bite and chew and swallow and take another bite. Curtis is quiet like always. But Brett had some kind of private talk with Coach this morning before school, and he's all fired up. As far as he's concerned, Coach is second only to God.

Brett's been talking all the way over, on and on about getting to state, about how to light a fire under the team this year. His mouth is still running like a faucet with the handle broken off, and you notice without really caring that Curtis is starting to throw glances of irritation his way. He always says Brett's mind is about three years behind his body, and Brett's mouth is another couple of years behind that.

". . . that's what Coach told me," Brett's saying. "He said how back when he was in high school the whole team would dogpile on the guy who screwed up the worst. And I thought: Now there's an idea. We could do that. Come on," he urges. "Y'all know it'd work, team spirit and all that. We could take state this year. You'd go for it, wouldn't you, Dobe, if you were playing?"

Dobie looks up from his half-eaten burger, still chewing. "Hmph?"

But Brett is a man with a mission. His voice gets louder and louder. "I know you got to agree, Hightower," he says, squirting ketchup in a puddle next to his fries. "Right? Whoever's got his head up his ass, the rest of us get to pound it out for him?"

"It's a stupid idea," Curtis says in a flat voice.

That turns Brett's faucet off. He drops the ketchup packet. In the sudden silence, Curtis adds, "That's where they came up with the phrase 'dumb jock'—because of ideas like that." He takes a bite of steak finger as Brett's face goes from tanned to white to red.

You're tired inside, but not too tired to see that things are heading downhill fast. Brett's got a temper like a firecracker. And Curtis couldn't care less that Brett's built like a Mack truck.

So, once again, it's up to you. You're going to have to click on that button. Only it won't quite click yet. "Don't be shy," you tell Curtis, trying to lighten the mood even though your smile's not working. "Tell us how you really feel."

"What's the matter?" Brett sneers at Curtis. "You scared you might be the one to get pounded?"

Curtis looks at Brett like he's a mosquito that's landed on his arm one too many times. "You really want to help us get to state, Stargill? Stop screwing around at practice."

Across the table, Dobie winces.

Brett's eyes narrow. "I don't screw around at practice."

"What do you call spitting ice chips at everybody? Mooning Dobie? Yelling at girls walking the track?"

"I call it none of your goddamn business."

"You're a distraction," says Curtis, as if he doesn't even see the way Brett's hands are starting to clench. "If anybody needs to have his head poun—"

Click. "I haven't seen any girls out there lately," you say, a little too loud. "Have you, Dobie?"

"Mrs. Hoskins," Dobie answers, shooting a worried glance from Curtis to Brett.

Not very helpful; Mrs. Hoskins is one of the PE teachers. Still, you take it and run with it. "Yeah, wearing those same old flappy shorts she's had for the past four years. But she sure did something different today," you add. "She flashed me when I walked past the bleachers."

It has the desired effect. Curtis, Brett, and Dobie all turn to look at you.

"She did not," Brett says.

"I swear. The top half, anyway. Just lifted up her blouse and showed me everything."

"Don't say that, Austin." Dobie looks horrified. "She's *old*. She could be your grandmother."

"You were dreaming, Reid." Brett makes an obscene gesture in his lap.

"Believe me," you say straight-faced, "it was no dream."

"Cut it out, Austin," Dobie insists. "She must be ninety years old."

Curtis just watches and listens. Doesn't say a word.

"Hey, I swear," you tell them. "The closest I can come

to describing it is two watermelons bouncing in a rubber hammock."

Stargill splutters and starts laughing. Dobie's face is about the color of a tomato.

You grin. The corners of Curtis's mouth are trying to rise up, but he won't let them.

"You lie," he finally says.

"Yeah," you agree.

Curtis's smile slips all the way out. He picks up an onion ring, shaking his head like he can't believe he calls you his best friend.

"Good thing she *didn't* flash you," Brett remarks, swooping a handful of fries in his ketchup. "You'd be scarred for life. Don't you know everything under there's got to be hanging like a used-up feed bag."

"I can't believe y'all are making fun of some old lady's private parts," Dobie says.

"Then why are you laughing?" Curtis asks.

"I didn't laugh."

"You smiled," Brett says through a mouthful of fries. "I saw you."

Now they're arguing about whether Dobie smiled or not, and you are no longer needed.

CHAPTER FOUR

Apparently God was trying to tell you something, the other night at the Dairy Queen. Because He says it again—and louder—that very afternoon.

Everybody sees Heather when she shows up at the very end of practice; everybody except Coach and Dobie. Dobie's got his head down; he's pounding equipment into a duffel bag at one end of the bleachers. Coach has his back to her as she comes down the hill toward the track; he's ending the session.

"Four more days till our first game," he's saying. Everybody's gathered in a bunch facing him—and Heather. "I like what I saw this afternoon. You keep it up to this level Friday, we'll stomp Burlington."

Heather walks past Dobie, who doesn't notice at first when she sits down at the other end of the bleachers, on the bottom row. She's wearing a skirt slit up the middle, and when she crosses her legs you're not the only player who turns to watch.

". . . no distractions," Coach is saying, while Heather lifts her arms to pull her hair up, away from her neck. She holds it there with one hand, back arched, fanning herself with the other hand. Her skintight sleeveless top pays a proper tribute to those gravity-defying breasts.

"I'm counting on you all to keep your head in it," Coach says.

Heather lets her hair fall back down around her shoulders, and recrosses her legs in the other direction. Both sides of the slit fall away.

Curtis is the only player who isn't looking at her now. Even Dobie has noticed. He stands stock-still, bent over the duffel bag, staring slack jawed down the bleachers at Heather as if he's forgotten what he's supposed to be doing.

"Keep up the good work," says Coach, holding out his hand, palm down. Everybody gathers around him in a circle, piling hands onto his. "Panthers . . . Go!" everybody shouts, and the huddle breaks up. Short and sweet.

Heather stands up.

Brett Stargill perks up as she steps out onto the field. "Watching practice?" he asks, strolling toward her.

"Not really," she says, not missing a beat as she passes him by and comes straight to you. "Hi, Austin."

Her eyes are locked onto yours. Your clothes are

soaked, your face streaming with sweat. You know you smell to high heaven.

"Melissa had to leave early today, and I don't have a ride. I was hoping you could give me one?"

Automatically, you flash her a grin. "Sure, if you don't mind waiting a few minutes. I kinda need to get cleaned up."

"You look fine to me." Her eyes flick up and down your sweat-soaked, grass-and-dirt-stained practice uniform; it reminds you of the way your mother used to check out the stance of a horse she wanted to buy. "Just fine. I really do appreciate this."

"Give me a couple minutes, and I'll be right out," you tell her easily—after all, this is Austin Reid's home territory.

"I'll just wait by your truck," she says, and gives you a smile before she turns away.

You watch her walk for a few moments, until you realize you're admiring the way her rear end sways and swings, the way her hair switches back and forth like a palomino's tail. And suddenly you feel like laughing, just when you thought you were completely shriveled up inside.

You turn around and go straight to the field house to get cleaned up, quick as you can.

"You're really thinking about asking her out, aren't you?" Curtis's voice is muffled by the T-shirt he's pulling on. "Even though she's got a heart about the size of a pea."

His head reappears out of the neck hole; he pulls the shirt all the way down and reaches for the belt hanging in his locker. He doesn't know that his words are like shotgun pellets trying to puncture you. And you hadn't understood exactly how light you were feeling, till he said that.

You shake out a slightly used sock, the one you wore to school, and start pulling it over your foot. "She's not that bad," you say in a low voice. "You don't really know her."

"Neither do you." Curtis threads his belt through the loops of his jeans.

"Nobody does," says Dobie from the other end of the lockers. He scoops up one damp towel from the floor and reaches for another. "Nobody under the age of eighteen, anyway. She only likes them college boys."

"I know her enough," Curtis says. "Every year she gets more and more picky about who she smiles at and who she speaks to. Except the week before the Homecoming Court gets elected. Then all of a sudden she's Miss Congeniality."

It's true, Heather's not real outgoing. True, too, that she can really turn it on when she wants something.

Today, it looks like she wants *you*.

"I'm not saying she doesn't *look* good," Curtis continues. "If you want to try to lay her, that's your choice. All I'm saying is, don't get all wrapped up in it."

Silence. Dobie reaches for another towel.

"Do I ever get wrapped up in it?" you hear yourself say, feel that grin flash across your face.

"No," says Curtis, his tone neither approving nor disapproving. "Look out, Dobe," he adds drily. "Here comes notch number twenty-seven."

"More like three hundred thirty-three," you kid, bending to tie your shoe. Actually it's more like number four—or five, depending on how you count.

"Notch?" Dobie asks.

"On his belt," Curtis explains. "He's exaggerating."

"Not by much," you say, and turn around and walk out to meet Heather.

"Don't worry, it'll cool down in here pretty soon," you tell her as you're easing the pickup out of the parking lot. "This old truck may not look like much, but it's got a good air conditioner."

Not exactly a sparkling topic. You try to think of something else, something that will at least open up a conversation. "So. You like football?"

"Yeah. Well, it's okay," she says doubtfully. "I mean, the actual game is just about *the* most boring thing in the universe. But I like the clothes. Like, the pads make you look all huge? And I like the way the pants fit." She says it so frankly that for a second you think you've heard wrong. "I can really tell who's in shape and who's not. I'll bet I can even tell who's a good player and who's not. Like that guy with the red hair you were standing next to—"

"Rhinehart?"

"Whatever. It's like, his pants are really saggy in the behind, which means he's probably real slow and clumsy."

"Well—"

"Whereas your pants fit nice and you've got good muscle tone, so I'm guessing you could really move out there, if you got hold of the ball. Am I right?"

She's right about Rhinehart. You think about her sitting on the bench, watching so intently when Coach gave his talk. Only it wasn't Coach she was watching.

"Are you blushing? Don't tell me; you thought only guys check out bodies. And you probably think only guys talk about them, too."

"I never really thought about it."

"Well, girls check out, and girls talk. Are you curious what we say about you?"

She's watching you with a little smile. Your fingers are gripping the steering wheel too tight; you flex them a little. "Not really," you tell her.

"Yes, you are. It's only human. Well, I'll tell you. The feeling around school is that you should model jeans or underwear or something."

Your face is hot. "Thanks for the info," you say, still able to make it come out casual.

"You're welcome." She doesn't seem to notice that the sides of her slit skirt just dropped open again, showing smooth, slender legs stretching clear up to Idaho. "On the other hand," she adds, "you're also known for not getting serious. Like you're working your way down a list?"

"I don't know what you've heard," you begin, trying to watch the road instead of her legs.

"Oh, I've heard enough. Now, tell me, how is practice going? It must be horrible out there in the sun."

"It's not so bad. Not like two-a-days."

"Two-a-days?"

"A couple of weeks before school starts, we work out twice a day. It's like cramming a month of workouts into two weeks. So we're out there pretty much all day."

"My goodness. Doing what?"

"Warm-ups. Lots of sprints—Coach is real big on speed. All kinds of drills. And we run plays, of course."

"Poor thing." Heather scrunches up her face in a sympathetic expression. "It must wear you out."

"Not too bad—not like last year," you add.

"Was it worse last year?"

"I could hardly walk the first couple of days. Felt like somebody'd beat on me with a two-by-four."

"Ooh. Sounds painful."

"It was. The morning after that first practice, I swear I couldn't even lift my feet off the floor." You don't add what Curtis said at the time, that he felt like an old man, the way he had to ease out of bed and shuffle into the bathroom to pee.

"Wow," says Heather. "But not this year?"

"No. We've been doing all right. Curtis talked me into lifting weights over the summer, and that probably kept us in shape some."

"Over the summer? You are *so* dedicated."

"Plus, I worked all summer. Maybe that helped."

"You've always looked in shape to me," Heather says. "Where did you work?"

"Winn-Dixie. I was a night stocker."

She asks about what night stockers do, about your family. You even find yourself telling her how Becky raises calves for 4-H, and she asks for more details.

It pumps you up a little, just having her here. You hardly ever talk about yourself—your friends already know all about you, and your girlfriends have always tended to talk about themselves.

Not to mention her legs, her body, her smile. It is a fact, she's drop-dead gorgeous. The most beautiful girl in town, all ears and hell-bent on getting to know you.

Heather's house is small, a painted white brick set far back from the street. The windows are shuttered from the inside. A long driveway edges past the house to an unattached garage at the back of the lot. You park in front and walk beside her up the sidewalk, boots clomping in time with the faint slap of her sandals.

On the concrete porch flanked by bushes on either side, you ask her. "Listen, I was wondering. Would you be interested in going out after the game Friday? If you don't mind meeting me at the field house. I could run in and get cleaned up real quick, after the bus brings us back."

"Hmm," she says. "I've got plans already. But the next Friday's open."

"Sure, that sounds good. Or this Saturday?" An extra week suddenly sounds awful long. Too long. "Saturday night, I mean. Unless you're busy then, too."

"No, Saturday sounds good."

So it's settled. "Well," you say, clicking on a smile—don't want to look like some loser hanging around, hoping for a kiss—"I guess I'll see you Saturday night, then."

She steps closer, and somehow—almost before all the words are out—she's sliding her arms around your neck at the same moment you're leaning forward, and you're in the middle of a kiss. And then your arms are pulling her even closer, and gradually it becomes a full-length, hip-pressing, tonsil-toucher of a kiss that wakes up all your nerve endings from the roots of your hair clear down to your toenails.

You can't help it, your hands slide down to her rear—and that's when she pulls away just enough to touch her lips—or is it her tongue?—to your ear. "I've always liked you, Austin." Her whisper sends prickles down your neck, and then she steps back, peeling off your arms like she's shedding old clothes.

She starts digging in her purse for her keys. "It took you long enough to ask me out," she says. "I thought I was going to have to hit you over the head or something."

She pulls out a huge key ring, almost big enough to drive your pickup through, and when she turns her back to open the door, you stuff your hands into your pockets just to make absolutely sure you keep them to yourself. Your eyes, however, take a long slow trip all over her.

Heather opens the door, but instead of going straight in like you expect, she hesitates. Then she squares her shoulders, turns around, and looks you straight in the eye. "It's going to be a good year," she informs you, then turns and walks inside.

All at once, you believe it.

The only sound is the turn of the deadbolt. The front door has a glass panel in the center, etched with designs. Just for a moment, you can see Heather behind the scrolls and curlicues. The next second, she disappears through a doorway to the right, and then all that's left is a living room—wooden floor, a couch, rugs scattered here and there, an armchair, pictures on the wall. Just a living room, like any other—but this one is Heather's, and down that hall to the right must be Heather's room, where she sleeps. In a bed. Mmm.

It's five whole days till Saturday. You do not want to leave this porch. You can almost smell her perfume lingering in the air, and you're not ready to stop floating on it.

You step off the porch and walk down that long sidewalk all by yourself. Getting into your truck is like slowly letting out a deep breath. You drive away, and everything inside you slowly deflates, till you're bumping along the road like a day-old balloon that wasn't quite ready to leave the ceiling.

CHAPTER FIVE

The first game is an away game.

In the locker room at the stadium, Cody Billings, the center, takes the offensive line off into a corner the way he always does; Coach wants the linemen to keep to themselves, like a family. A few of the other guys are still messing around, but most are starting to get serious. Brett Stargill bangs his head rhythmically against the wall the way he always does to get himself pumped. Jason Cox leans against the same wall, helmet under his arm, eyes shut, oblivious to the crash and thunder next to him. Dobie edges past both of them with a roll of white tape, not wanting to disturb their rituals.

You do what you always do: walk around and around, more from habit than anything else. You don't have those butterflies that always take flight in your stomach just before a game. You can't feel a single one fluttering inside. It's as if they're all dead, and all that's left is their weight in the pit of your stomach.

Curtis sits on a bench next to the water fountain. He's already off in whatever world he goes to before a game. On the bus and in the locker room, he likes to keep himself apart, likes to build his concentration to a pinpoint that'll knock anybody to their knees if they happen to get in its way. Right now he has his helmet on, chin strap in place, and he's leaning forward as if praying, elbows on knees as he stares at the floor between his feet.

You walk along the benches, around the free-standing lockers, and back. Placing each foot precisely on the floor—because that's what you always do, because you're always careful to keep the lid on, to keep all that energy trapped inside, ready to be unleashed at the right place and the right time. You can't feel it tonight, but surely it's there. Isn't it? Way underneath?

On your third trip around the room, you stop to get a drink of water. Curtis is still sitting next to the fountain, but he doesn't look up. You're not sure he even knows you're there. You straighten to wipe your mouth on your sleeve.

It's scary, to feel nothing. What if you never feel anything again?

There Curtis sits, steady and calm as always. It makes you feel better for a moment just to be in the same room with him.

"A long time ago," Curtis says to the floor, "when a guy was about to become a knight, he spent the whole night before getting purified. You know, like baths and prayer and getting dressed in ceremonial clothes. And the next morning, when they were about to have the ceremony itself, he'd have all his friends around, helping him to get armed. It was like a ritual."

He raises his head then, and looks at you.

"Everything," he says, "had to be done exactly right. First, the guy had to be one of the chosen. He had to have the ability, and the desire. He had to be ready on the outside—and then he had get ready on the *inside*." Curtis pauses. "He'd use the time before the ceremony to get ready. You know what I'm saying?"

You nod. For Curtis, football is a moment of single-minded purity that last four quarters.

"And then," he continues, "at the very last, he could put on his clothes and his armor and his weapons. And then he could become a knight."

He stops as Coach comes in and calls everyone together. You look around the locker room, at everybody. Ankles taped, some right over the cleats. Wristbands and gloves. Pads strapped on. Snowy white socks and pants, and over them, the bright purple jerseys. Face masks like visors.

When Coach has everyone's full attention, he begins.

"I want everybody playing hard for sixty minutes.

Don't let up on these guys. Don't even think about stopping till after you hear that whistle. I expect every one of you to play four full quarters of football.

"Make all your tackles. Make your catches. Follow through on your blocks. Defensive ends, cornerbacks: Don't let any sweeps get outside of you. Contain, contain, contain!

"If I catch anybody making any mistakes, they'd better at least be doing it at full speed. You all clear on that?"

"Yes, sir!" everyone shouts on cue.

"I have never lost a season opener." Coach's voice echoes around the locker room. "Not as a player. Not as a coach. That is not going to change tonight."

His words fall, coming to rest in absolute quiet.

"Now, we're going to have a moment of silent thought."

Coach folds his hands in front of him. Heads bow. You take another slow look around, at the helmets and pads, like armor.

Even Curtis's head is down. You bow your head and stare at the floor. You visualize the scene:

The ball's sailing right at you. Your hands are up and open, fingers spread. You watch the ball all the way into your hands. Wrap it up. Take off running.

You play the scene again. And once more. You've always had the ability to be the best. Tonight, you've got the desire. It's not like last year—still no butterflies. But you do want to be the best.

"Amen," says Coach. The room rustles as everyone prepares to head for the field.

"Amen," you agree. For once, you're feeling down-right hopeful.

The first touchdown of the season is yours.

First quarter, 0–0, and Stargill's just picked up a first down—not much pressure, not yet. It's long and out, just like at practice, and when you turn to look at Cox, the ball's heading toward the exact spot you'll be in a second. You don't think at all, just stretch out till your fingers feel the firm scrape of pigskin. You tuck it in and run twenty-five yards, the final ten free and clear.

Last year, you scored fifteen touchdowns. After each you were so pumped you almost danced off the ground, raising your arms and yelling with the crowd. Last year, every little success sent you spiraling into the night air, high above the stadium.

Tonight, your feet cross the line and you feel nothing.

Smack! Brett Stargill has hurled himself at you. Helmet meets shoulder pads and you find yourself being hugged, faceless, into purple cloth. Brett pounds your back in a wordless frenzy. You can hear the shouts of joy from the field, the cheers from the stands.

You suppose you might be smiling. Then again, you

might not be. Hard to tell, when you're not feeling anything at all.

You drop the ball onto the turf and start walking back.

This was supposed to be the very best moment of the game. The first of a long line of best moments—the best of the season, maybe even your life.

When you get to the sidelines, Coach gives you a friendly slap across the helmet. "That's it, Reid," he says, "that's the way."

Coach seldom gives compliments, so you should be pleased. But his words skitter on the surface and float away, meaningless.

As soon as the extra point clears the uprights, the fight song comes blasting out of the band, too fast, as if somebody spiked the concession stand Cokes with adrenaline.

You barely hear it. You keep your helmet on. Keep your back to the stands. Watch the kickoff like it's something that's happening on TV.

The Panthers win, 21–17. But at the team meeting the next morning, Coach doesn't seem to have noticed that fact.

"I couldn't hardly sleep last night," he says, plopping the game tape into the VCR. "Burlington's got the worst offense in the district, and we gave 'em seventeen points.

We come up against a real team, we're going to get plowed."

You're sitting there, attacked by the usual day-after-a-game soreness. Your muscles are stiff; your shoulders ache, and the backs of your thighs. Every once in a while your left ankle gets one of those twinges that feels like somebody's tightening a screw in it.

"Looky there how high Billings comes out," Coach says as he points to the screen. "See how he gets brushed off? Billings, you know better than that. I know you know better. Palmer, you got to pay attention to where that marker is. We should've had a first down right here."

Inside you're still feeling nothing, but it doesn't seem so important now. Your body will keep doing what it's supposed to do, at the time it's supposed to do it. And everything will just keep moving around you, no matter what.

"Kemp, you have too much coffee before the game? That's twice you let that guy draw you offsides. Twice! All he had to do was twitch his nose, and there you go."

It's impossible to get interested in game films.

All there is of Curtis are his long legs stretched out on the other side of Stargill. He's sprawled in his chair, his attention on last night's game.

"You guys on the offensive line have to give Cox more time," Coach is saying. "Hernandez, you're giving up too soon—keep driving till you hear the whistle. Nice run there, Reid," Coach adds, and sure enough, there's number 83 on the screen. That's you.

The tape rolls on. Every once in awhile Coach pauses it, hits rewind. Your eyes stay on the screen now, on number 83. He's physical proof that you were there last night. And it's good to have the aches and pains pinning you into your body. Otherwise you feel you might just disappear, sink through the floor with the air closing over your head as you dropped. All the chairs would come together to fill the space where you once had been.

"Now, what the hell was this, Rhinehart?" Freeze frame on Rhinehart of the saggy pants, caught in bewildered mid-lope, yards behind a guy he can never catch up with. "You look like you're playing flag football at the Y! I've never seen so many mental errors in my life," Coach announces. "When I was in high school, I would've rather died than made some of the screwups you guys pulled last night. It didn't take a whole staff of coaches barking at us to keep us in gear. We took care of our own business."

"Dogpile," Brett Stargill says under his breath. His eyes are lit up; words are one thing, but pounding is something Brett understands.

"We kept our own heads in the game," Coach says.

"Dogpile," Brett says again, a little louder.

Coach gives him a sharp look. "You coaching this team, Stargill?"

"No, sir."

"Then shut up." Coach stands in the middle of the room, staring at nothing with furrowed brow. He sighs and rubs his forehead as if there's too much going on in his head to even attempt to explain.

Then he looks across the room at Stargill, who wears his feelings on his face. At Cody Billings, who talks trash on the field then holds his own in a fight. At Ryan Hernandez, who explodes with each snap of the ball. "All right," he says, almost to himself, and then he announces loud and clear: "Come Monday morning, we're going to have a new drill. It's time to get serious, gentlemen."

Rhinehart sits with his eyes straight ahead, his pudgy cheeks splotched red and white. Curtis is sitting up straight now; Curtis who has been serious about football from the first time he put on a uniform back in third grade, in the recreational league.

You started playing football at the same time as Curtis. But number 83 is not on the screen right now, because he wasn't on the field at this point last night. And right now you don't feel that you're anywhere at all.

"It's going to be a good year." Coach adds firmly, like he's going to *make* it be a good year by sheer force of will.

It's going to be a good year.

Something flickers inside you. The last time you heard those words was on Heather's front porch.

You are going out with Heather tonight.

The thought has lain there since Monday afternoon, like a seed. Now it's Saturday, and while everybody else is getting serious about football, that seed flutters to life.

I've always liked you, Austin.

The tape rolls on. The screen becomes a blur of swaying lines and battling bodies again. Faceless, like ants. Not one of them is as real as the tickle of Heather's breath in your ear.

CHAPTER SIX

You pick Heather up early in the evening. You'll take her to dinner first, then a movie.

While you're waiting for her to answer the doorbell, you look around Heather's neighborhood with its neat streets, its tidy yards shoved tight together. It makes your neighborhood seem downright shabby, with yards and pastures patched together not by concrete driveways, but by barbed-wire fences or white plank fences or no fences at all; brick houses neighboring wood houses neighboring trailers.

Then Heather opens the door, and you forget all about feeling shabby. When she walks down the sidewalk next to you, her perfume brushes against you like light, teasing fingers. It's not flowers or spices, but the kind of thing you'd expect from a girl who went to the prom last year in a short little black strapless dress that made every guy there wish it'd ride up just a few more inches. Or else fall down just half an inch.

You breathe a little deeper to catch the scent again.

Once the truck's moving, you guess you wouldn't mind putting your arm around her—she's sitting in the center of the seat, right next to you—but you know from experience you'll have to move your arm every time you shift gears. And once when you did that, you conked your date in the back of her head with your elbow.

So you let your right hand rest on your thigh, though it's actually sort of wanting to move over to hold Heather's hand, fine boned and delicate, with its pale silvery polish.

"I heard you guys had a great game last night," she's saying. "I was sorry I couldn't be there. But still. Congratulations."

"Thanks. You coming next Friday?"

"Mm-hmm. Even got a new top for it. A black knit shell—it'll look good with jeans. I haven't decided about the matching cardigan—it's got short sleeves and all, but I don't want to get too hot. And of course I'll wear my new sandals."

She's not asking for your opinion, but you nod, anyway. She smiles at you. There's a love song playing on the radio. You really like having her here next to you, but you can't think of anything to say. It doesn't seem to matter. Heather radiates contentment, satisfaction, self-esteem. It's almost as if you're huddled next to a campfire, enjoying its warmth.

And that trickle of interest is flowing, the one that's always pulled you to Heather. Even though you don't even know the small stuff about her, like whether she goes to church or what kind of music she likes. Or what her favorite color is. Or whether she can tell a zone defense from man-to-man. The only thing you know is that she doesn't have any brothers or sisters. And you know where her house is and what it looks like.

And you know about her dad.

"You live with your mom, don't you?" you ask.

"Yeah." She glances at the radio. "Hey. Do you mind if we listen to some *real* music?" She doesn't wait for you to answer, just reaches for the buttons and starts clicking her way down the dial. You almost admire her. Heather doesn't need anybody's approval.

"Put on anything you like," you tell her.

Dance music blares from the speakers. Heather's finger hovers over the button for a second, then she sits up; the dance music must meet with her favor. "What about your parents? Are they still together?"

"No." It's been awhile since you've said this next part. "My dad's dead," you tell her, ready for Heather to catch your words up and carry them forward. Maybe she'll turn to you in complete understanding, and say: "Really? My dad's dead, too."

The only sound is the drone of rubber on asphalt. When you glance over, she's staring out the window—only there's not much scenery on this stretch of 171.

"What did he die from?" she asks after a moment.

"Cancer," you say, glancing at her again.

"What kind?"

Okay. She wants you to share first. Well, you've been through this part before. It's always kind of awkward; this is the part where you're supposed to tell your story. You try to oblige. "It was cancer of the esophagus," you begin. "He died when I was three," you finish.

There's no middle to the story, because you don't remember him. There's nothing else to tell.

When you glance over to check Heather's reaction, she's watching you, her gaze straight and unwavering as she waits for the middle of your story.

You have to look away, clear your throat. Reach to turn the radio up. "This's a good song," you mention, careful to keep your eyes on the road.

You can't tell her how you used to play at shaving, because that's stupid. No way you could tell her about sitting on the bathroom counter in your pajamas. Or that your father was the one who taught you to shave, even though he was long gone at the time.

When you were fourteen, you had a few whiskers that you thought needed to come off, so you went and bought a can of gel foam. When you got home you locked yourself in the bathroom and pulled out the wooden box that held your dad's old-fashioned safety razor, the one you'd found tucked away in the back of the medicine cabinet, gathering dust. Mom, never one to be sentimental, had forgotten about it. She said you could have it if you wanted, that it'd been a gift from somebody—she couldn't remember who—to your father a long time ago. It looked like a gift; gold plated, lying on red velvet.

Then you pulled the can out of the sack. On the back were the directions: *Leave skin wet. Put gel on fingertips. Gently rub over skin to lather and shave.*

It didn't say anything about what to do with the sink—but you already knew. You remembered very clearly how the sink was filled with warm water. You could almost hear the *dabble-dabble-shake* of the razor. You could almost see your dad's hand holding it, strong and big and forever.

You're driving along, not really seeing the road ahead of you, remembering all this. Your right hand is resting on the seat next to your thigh, and you're vaguely aware of Heather touching the class ring on your finger, as if she's looking at it, but you don't really start to pay attention until she begins to stroke the back of your hand. It's a light touch, but slow and deliberate, and after a moment or two it begins to set off nerve endings that reach way beyond the area she's touching.

You try to concentrate on watching the road. She

slides her hand under yours, interlaces her fingers with yours, and lifts the whole thing to her lips. "No sadness allowed," she says, very low, and you glance at her as she kisses the very tip of your index finger. It looks like she's tasting a drop of honey. You hear a quick intake of breath.

It came from you.

A horn blares, the center line disappears under the hood—your pickup is drifting into the oncoming lane. You jerk your hand away from Heather and swerve back again.

Both hands are on the steering wheel now. Your heart is going like a jackhammer, whether from having your fingertip sucked or from almost being killed there's no telling. You have to pull over into the next parking lot that comes along. You can't think.

When you turn to ask Heather if she's okay, she's looking across the lot . . . at the sign that says Giacotti's Pizza and Spaghetti.

"Why are you stopping way back here? There's a spot right in front."

No indication she realizes she just gave you a boner that could steer the truck all by itself.

Inside Giacotti's, you order the pizza while Heather selects a booth to sit in. You want to slide in to sit beside her—you've always thought people who did that were stupid, facing straight ahead, bumping shoulders and elbows. But tonight you think you'd like it, even as you take the seat across from her.

Heather calls some of her friends over; they stand gathered at the edge of the booth in the dim light, saying hi with big smiles, while Heather smiles even bigger. When they finally leave, Heather shakes back her hair and says: "We make a cute couple, don't you think?"

Whatever that was, back in the truck, it's over. Gone. Completely. When she looks at you her eyes are clear blue and completely blank.

"I always thought your hair was black, but really it's dark brown, isn't it? Anyway, we're a good contrast," she continues, as if she's talking about a color wheel. She removes the wrapper from her straw. "Being as I'm blond and all. And the top of my head probably comes just about to your chin. Don't you think?"

"Yeah," you say, wondering what difference it makes. "I guess."

"So we're just about the perfect heights for everything. Pictures. Kissing. Sex."

She says it matter-of-factly, like checking off a list. But it drives the breath from your lungs.

"Do you think I've got a nice body?" she asks, sliding her straw into the glass.

"Yes." The word comes out a little hoarse.

"Thanks." She sips her drink, and you watch the way

her lips close around the straw, and the way her breasts almost rest on the table as she leans forward. You're not sure how you feel about all this talk about looks. You *are* sure how you feel when she talks about sex, right up front like that. How you felt when she sucked on your finger.

Lighten up. Be joyful always.

God sure does work in mysterious ways.

After the movie you figure you'll drive down by the railroad tracks. They're easy to get to; down an unmarked farm road leading off the main highway.

But the moment you hit the blinker to turn right, Heather sits straight up, like she's been shot. "Where are you going?"

"Where there's a little privacy."

"Sorry. I don't do the parking thing on a first date."

She's got to be kidding.

You look over at her; one of her hands is flat on the seat beside her. The other is gripping the door handle.

She's not kidding.

Better double-check. "You mean you want me to take you straight home?"

"Yeah."

Yeah. All right. Fine.

She's a tease. And this particular kind of dishonesty always did hit you like a shot of ice water, straight to the bone.

You zip your lip, turn off the blinker, and hit the gas.

You know the drill by heart. If not this night, then maybe the next. Or the next. Or the next. And if not, there's always the next girl.

A couple miles of silence later, when you pull up in front of her house, you don't make a move to touch her. Just get out, walk around, and open her door. Escort her up the sidewalk. On the front porch, you just flash her a grin and give her a quick kiss good-bye. No hands. "I'll call you," you tell her without meaning it. The usual.

Heather's smile drops off her face. "You'll *call* me," she echoes, as if she can't believe she heard you right.

"Yeah," you say automatically. "I've got your number. I'll call you sometime."

"*Sometime,*" she repeats in that flat, thoughtful tone, then peers at you in the dim light. "No. I think not. I'm not some little football groupie who sits at home, pining for a phone call."

You don't know what to say to that. She doesn't seem angry. Just a little puzzled. Like you're some new type of butterfly she can't quite pin to the board.

"I would like to go out with you again," she says with a slight frown. When you still don't say anything, she adds slowly: "Like, maybe next weekend?" Another pause. "Oh, my God." Her eyes widen, horrified. "I just asked you for a date." Even in the dim light of the porch you can see that her cheeks are turning red. "I don't do that. I don't ask guys out. God," she says, and puts both hands over her face, "I'm gonna die."

"Don't die," you tell her, trying not to laugh. "It's all right."

"No, it's not," she says, her voice muffled.

You stand there for a while; she keeps her face hidden behind her fingers. "Really, it's okay," you tell her. "How about Friday night, after the game?"

"I guess so."

Finally she lowers her hands. Her face is red, clear up to the roots of her hair. "It's not that big a deal," you tell her.

"It is to me. I have never, ever, had to ask a guy out."

"Can't say that next time," you tell her gently, and she looks at you for a moment before a smile rises up her face, slight and slow.

"It's too bad you're a guy. I get the feeling we could have been good friends."

A laugh bursts out before you realize she's not kidding. "It *is* possible to be friends with a guy."

"I think not."

"Sure it is," you tell her.

Now it's Heather's turn to laugh. "You really are this decent, nice person, aren't you? That could be a problem," she adds, stepping closer. "I *like* people who are nice, but I never quite know what to *do* with them."

She slides her arms around your neck. And then she's kissing you.

And suddenly everything's exactly what you expected, and this time she lets you squeeze her to you for a few moments before she pushes you away.

"Ohmigod," she says breathless. "You are too much. I'm going in now. Call me, okay?"

"Okay. Tomorrow," you add with a grin. "I've never, ever, called a girl the next day. So we'll be even."

She doesn't say anything, just digs in her purse for that oversize key ring. "By the way," she says, without looking up, "I was really glad you got junior favorite last year. I voted for you."

You don't say anything. She pauses, then looks up at you, as if waiting for something.

"Thanks," you tell her, and she bestows one of those beauty queen smiles as a reward.

Driving away a few moments later, you're thinking that there are two Heathers, and the outer one is like a paper doll, all propped up with a painted-on face. You should know, you keep yourself propped up, too.

You remember Curtis's warning. If it's your choice, sure, you're going to try to lay that girl with the beauty queen smile. But the girl underneath—the girl with the flushed cheeks and the embarrassed smile—well, you can see where it wouldn't be hard to get at least a little wrapped up in her.

63

CHAPTER SEVEN

The next morning is Sunday. Sunday always gathers its own momentum; you just catch hold and ride along. You walk into church with that smile clicked on; surely it will soak in if it's on your face long enough. Be joyful always—right?

But when you sit down the smile is already trying to fade. You prop up the corners of your mouth and look around the sanctuary; you've sat here every Sunday you can remember. The sun comes in through tall stained-glass windows on the side walls, making patches on the floor like pieces in some colorful puzzle. When you were little you'd tell Mom you wanted to sit on the side aisle, just so you could stretch a hand out in the dim light of the sanctuary and spread your fingers to feel the warm colors pouring over your palm.

But you're not sitting on the aisle now. And you're not little anymore. The pews are hard, and dark with age, and the air is musty with old varnish.

The only thing that's light is the thought of Heather. You're pretty sure the two of you have something in common, something about having seen underneath the skin of the world while most other people think the outside is all there is. Although, to be honest, it's hard to think about Heather *without* thinking about her outside, since she comes wrapped in so fine a package.

Very fine.

But this is not the place for those kinds of thoughts. Time to stand and sing. Becky holds the hymn book out so the two of you can share. You don't sing, just read along with the words.

Did we in our own strength confide
Our striving would be losing;
Were not the right Man on our side,
The Man of God's own choosing. . . .

Curtis and his mother are sitting two rows up. They don't look much alike, even from the back. Gayle Hightower is short and faded and homey looking, while Curtis takes after his dad, tall and whip thin. He's got on his usual sports shirt. No tie. His mom's probably just glad he doesn't wear jeans to church.

You've tried not wearing a tie, but you've never made it out the door without getting caught, nagged, and harped on. Mom wouldn't care if the preacher himself declared casual day—to her it's bad enough you don't wear a suit. She says dressing up is a sign of respect to God. You believe God looks inside people, not at what they're wearing, but you don't figure He'd appreciate you arguing with your mother about it, either.

He also wouldn't appreciate the way your mind keeps hearing Heather's voice, saying the two of you are the perfect heights for sex.

So you make yourself notice how Becky is singing under her breath. That's what she does lately. Must be some girl thing, like throwing a fit over who gets to use the phone, or screeching when you accidentally pull a box of girl stuff—*supplies*—out of the grocery bag. You kind of miss her singing. There was something light and sweet about her voice. Plus, when she doesn't sing, everybody can hear your mother that much better. Mom never could carry a tune, but that doesn't make her lower *her* voice one decibel. She just stands there singing in her trademark half croak, half bleat, wearing her Sunday dress that Becky picked out for her because she says Mom shouldn't wear a suit to church, but Mom won't make time to shop for dresses.

That word above all earthly pow'rs,
No thanks to them, abideth. . . .

Everybody but you and Becky is singing. The words rise straight up around you, faithful and unblinking.

You've completely lost your place on the page now. With nothing to nail your eyes to, it's hard not to remember how Heather kissed your finger last night—well, not kissed, not exactly. To be accurate, you'd have to call it sucking. No—more than sucking, actually, because you are fairly positive that Heather used her tongue. Fingertips are very sensitive, and there was definitely a split second where something more than sucking was going on; something soft and fluttery and wet.

Of course, it's not right—thinking about sucking. Not here.

So you look at Curtis's back and think about the Hightowers. Used to be, Mr. Hightower stood on the other side of Mrs. Hightower. Not anymore; five years ago he ran off with that intern.

You met her once. Her name was Tiffani with an *i*, and even though you were only twelve, you could see why somebody would want to run off with her. Of course, you met her before the divorce, before anybody knew what was going on. She wasn't much older than you are now, and pretty, too, in a vivid flowery dress that didn't seem to belong in Mr. Hightower's dull gray office. You made some stupid twelve-year-old joke, and she threw back her head and laughed a bright, frilly laugh that didn't belong in that office, either. She was blond and curvy and young—not at all like Mrs. Hightower.

More like Heather, actually.

But Heather's prettier.

You look down at the hymnal, not really seeing it, trying to remember Tiffani's face. All you can picture is Heather's—but it doesn't fit with the dress Tiffani wore that day. You don't know why, but you can't imagine Heather Mackenzie wearing something with a lot of splashy colors. Not that she'd wear some prim dress with a bow at the neck, either—you've never seen her in anything like some of these dresses in the pews around you. In fact, Heather doesn't seem like the church type at all. You'd bet cold hard cash she's at home right this minute. Even still in bed, maybe.

Now *there's* a picture. Heather in bed. You can't quite see her in pajamas. Maybe in a pajama *top*. Or some clingy thing with thin little shoulder straps, her hair spilling over her bare back the way it spilled over her cheeks when she sucked your finger in the truck last night.

> *Let goods and kindred go,*
> *This mortal life also;*
> *The body they may kill*
> *God's truth abideth still. . . .*

You suddenly hear the words you're supposed to be singing. You realize your mind keeps wandering to some mortal things. Very mortal. In *church*.

His kingdom is forever.
Ahhhh-mehhhn.

The sanctuary fills with that rustling, collapsing sound made by a bunch of people sitting down at the same time. You sit down, too, a moment late.

Here you are thinking yourself into horniness, and in the one place on earth where you're supposed to have a clean and pure heart.

I'm sorry, you tell God, and wait for Him to answer— the way He used to answer your prayers, with a feeling of peace.

Nothing happens.

Of course not. The things you fail at are things inside, things that nobody but God sees. Things you couldn't explain to anybody—like wallowing around in bed for hours when everybody else just gets up. Like moping around when you're supposed to shake it off and be joyful. Keeping conversations light when they should get serious. Staying quiet when you should speak up. Having another beer when you should quit for the night. Putting your hands all over some girl when you should keep them to yourself.

A million things you screw up, and to top it off, now you're thinking lustful thoughts in the house of the Lord.

". . . because of his defect," the preacher is saying, in

that rich voice that means he's reading the words of God, "he must not go near the curtain or approach the altar, and so desecrate My sanctuary. I am the Lord, who makes them holy."

You feel yourself shiver. Becky glances at you; you ignore her. I'm sorry, you tell God again. He's still not answering.

You can't say that you blame Him.

CHAPTER EIGHT

That night you dream you're driving the pickup with Heather sitting next to you. But in the dream, she's not on the passenger side, she's sitting in the center, pressed warm against you, so close that she has one foot resting on either side of the stick shift. She's wearing a very short skirt.

You have to reach between her legs to grab the stick. You feel the hum under your foot as you press the gas pedal, powering up the engine, everything starts rolling, then, ahh! you thrust the stick between those slender thighs, into second gear. The engine thrums louder, you grip the knob in your palm, slide the stick out to third gear, let the throbbing build again and . . . ahh! in to fourth.

That's when the alarm goes off and you wake up, sweaty and trembling. All through the morning your body—brain included—seems to be vibrating at a higher frequency than usual. A Heather-frequency. It's not bad at all, like a low, pleased hum that carries you into the day, and it doesn't wear off completely till afternoon practice.

That's when Coach reveals his new drill.

Dobie's already on the other end of the field, setting up cones to mark the turnaround point for sprints. On this end of the field, Coach tells everybody to fasten their chin straps. He tells everybody to get in a circle. Which everyone does, joking around, taking their time.

"Not you, Rhinehart," Coach says. "Get in the middle."

Rhinehart obediently steps into the center of the circle, stands waiting. "Oh, boy," Jason Cox cracks. "'Farmer in the Dell.' Do we get to hold hands?" Stargill snickers.

Coach ignores them both. "This is our new drill. When I was in school, they called this Bull-in-a-Ring." He picks up his whistle. "Rhinehart, I know this don't seem fair because you only had a few minutes play Friday. But since you gave the most bonehead performance, you get to start us off.

"Now listen up, men," Coach announces to everyone in the circle. "When I point to you, it's your turn to try to knock him down. I want to see some good form. Good, solid hits. Don't wrap him up, just take him off his feet if you can. Then get out of the way, quick. Rhinehart, get those feet moving! Don't watch me—keep your eyes moving, too! I guarantee you don't know where it's going to come from. Everybody down. Set."

Coach blows his whistle at the same instant he points to Curtis—but Curtis hesitates.

Coach motions from him to Rhinehart.

Curtis ducks his head and drives straight into Rhinehart. It's like taking down a sack of flour. Rhinehart's back hits the ground with a *whoof!* You almost expect to see dust rising around him.

Curtis gets to his feet, holds a hand out to help Rhinehart up.

Coach removes the whistle from his mouth. "This ain't a cotillion," he says. "Hightower, get out of the way. Rhinehart, shake it off! Get your ass up off the ground and get ready for the next one."

Curtis goes back to his place in the circle. His mouth is a tight line. Curtis is usually all cold maneuvers on any field, but he doesn't like this drill, and when you look at him across the circle, his eyes are taking on that angry look you've only seen once or twice—something he cares about is being tainted, and he's ready to tear into it and peel the stains off with his bare hands. Only this time, he can't. There's nothing he can do about this.

Sometimes Coach sends them one at a time, sometimes two. From all places around the circle, from all directions, and Rhinehart in the middle, staggering to his feet each time like a wounded moose.

73

When Coach blows the whistle and points to you, you try not to think about it at all. You just blast off your stance, drive up and into Rhineheart, like you've been taught since third grade.

It's almost like plowing into one of those blow-up punching-bag clowns. Only this one doesn't pop immediately back up; it stands up very, very slowly.

Over Rhinehart's shoulder, yards away, Dobie has stopped working. Usually he keeps pretty busy, but now he's just watching the drill, holding the stack of orange cones that he's supposed to be putting out.

When it's all over, Rhinehart isn't really hurt. He walks a little funny as he heads off to get in line for sprints, but he doesn't complain—just shuffles away and you see that his eyes are a little red, but that's something you're not supposed to see. No one is supposed to see that. So you shove down the strange sorrow that's pricking the back of your throat, and you silently trudge over to get in line along with Rhinehart.

Bull-in-a-Ring works. Nobody's messing around now. Even Dobie is acting like his life depends on getting each cone placed to the inch. Nobody straggles or tosses off jokes. Everybody zips through the drills like Coach is yapping at their heels. And Coach is smiling, and practice is really clicking, moving along like clockwork with every piece well greased and in place.

When the time comes for running plays, you bend

down into your stance, and there is Curtis, still angry, looking hard and fierce across the line at whatever is opposing him.

Which happens to be you. It could be anybody, standing here on this particular day. But it's you, and every time you take off you can feel Curtis on your heels, his eyes burning holes through your head. He's ready to pull you down like a wolf pulls down a deer, only this wolf's going to ram your face into the dirt instead of ripping out your entrails.

So you try to hurry, try to get the ball wrapped up a little more quickly, get moving a little sooner, but somehow everything is just a little *off*. Your hands keep coming up empty. Incomplete pass.

Incomplete.

Incomplete.

"What the hell is going on?" Coach's voice bawls across the practice field. "Hey! Pride of the Panthers! I'm talking to you!"

Surprised, you look over. Coach's eyes are on you. Cox is watching. And Billings. And Stargill's looking at you, Stargill who's been popping up off the ground after every play, like the grass would burn him if he didn't.

Everybody is looking at you.

Coach shifts the wad in his cheek, like he's thinking. "You're hearing footsteps, Reid," he finally points out.

Hearing footsteps. You know what that means, of

course. Sometimes when a player's about to make a catch, he feels the defender breathing down his neck. Knowing he's about to get hit makes him lose his concentration. And very often, the ball.

"Keep focused, son," Coach warns. "Wrap that ball up tight before you even think about moving."

"Yes, sir."

"You get in a game and drop a catchable ball, come Monday you might just wish you'd died trying." He deliberately lets his gaze fall on Rhinehart, whose sweaty, already-red face gets even redder. Your shoulders hunch a little. You feel naked and visible, as if the propped-up paper doll that was you has been blown away during the course of this afternoon.

After practice, Rhinehart lumbers into the locker room more slowly than usual, but otherwise he doesn't seem to feel any ill effects from having his head pounded out of his ass. Dobie's still outside, collecting the rest of the equipment. All the guys are laughing, messing around like every other practice.

Except Curtis. Sitting on the bench next to you, he pulls his shirt off in one quick, angry movement, over his head.

"I think Coach just wanted us to learn something," you offer.

"I didn't learn anything. Just helped beat the crap out

of Rhinehart." Curtis says it matter-of-factly. But when he takes off his cleats he hurls them into the bottom of his locker, sending chips of dried mud flying.

You don't try again. You sit there for a moment, half undressed on the bench in front of your open locker. Your practice jersey lies crumpled on the floor, waiting to be exchanged for a clean, already laundered one. Your shoulder pads sit passive, your helmet hangs empty, and you think how the players have been provided with all this equipment to keep them from getting hurt. How the whole school district plans and pays to keep the players safe—at the same time that all of you are trying to pulverize each other into dust.

That's what you did to Rhinehart; you hit him so hard that he couldn't even get up right away. You get out there and hurt somebody like Rhinehart and then walk off without even caring, because that's what the Pride of the Panthers does.

You have to admit that you don't like this game much anymore. You used to like it; it made you feel good. But somehow football's become just another one of all the things you used to enjoy that got swallowed up. It almost hurts, if you think about how many things you used to enjoy.

"You going to tell Coach he's a dumb jock with a stupid idea, Hightower?" Brett Stargill jeers on his way to the showers. He snaps a towel inches away from

Curtis's neck as he passes by, not noticing or caring that Curtis doesn't flinch.

"It's supposed to be a sport," Curtis says under his breath. "Not a torture session."

You make yourself stand up. With that movement, your hand rises and begins to unlace your dirt-streaked pants. It pulls the pads out and tosses them on top of your cleats. All on its own.

It starts to rain as you pull out of the field house parking lot. The wet-asphalt smell, the sodden air, the miserable afternoon—they all add up to a tightness in your lungs that makes it difficult to breathe deeply. Like some weird bubble is pressing up against the inside of your chest.

Out on 171 you stop for a red light; the engine dies down to a low drone. The wipers pump back and forth. You notice that your fingers are numb; it's because they're squeezing the steering wheel. Your blood has given up trying to make its way into those too-tight fists and is hurrying back to the heart to get air.

What you really want to do is give up trying, too. Lay your head down on the steering wheel and quit squeezing, quit breathing, quit trying.

The problem is, you can't. Just quit, that is. When people want to quit, they have to choose. Make a decision. Take action.

If it was you who had to quit, you wouldn't pick guns

or pills. You'd pick your dad's razor. After all, he wasn't that much older than you are when he died.

It would make a mess to do it properly—cut toward the palm instead of across the wrist. You don't remember where you read that, how people try to kill themselves and end up alive with severed tendons.

The truck idles. The wipers fight to keep your view clear. Just ahead, in the drizzle, a street sign says Keller Avenue. You've stared at it for a while before you really see it—and then you realize where you are.

A right turn will take you toward Heather's house.

Everything inside you shifts a little. Decisions hang off somewhere in the distance, like a little cloud that you can't quite see. And won't have to see, if you just turn right.

A car honks behind you—the light's green.

You cut the wheel and turn. Your fingers must have loosened a little; they start to tingle.

Your hands know all the turns by heart; your feet know just when to brake and when to accelerate.

In front of the Mackenzies' house, you kill the engine and just sit for a few moments. The blades of grass are bright green in the slackening rain. The long driveway that edges past the house is spattered with puddles.

Heather's house.

A small house. Shutters inside windows, closed. The concrete porch where she kissed you good night.

You pull the door handle and slide out of the truck. The air is steamy hot. Drops plop on your neck and face. Your feet stride around to the curb, carry you all the way up the sidewalk. Two steps up to the porch, and you're standing in front of the door. Your finger presses the doorbell, and after a few moments the door opens.

For a split second you don't recognize Heather; you catch a flash of big startled eyes, but everything else is a very un-Heatherish impression—oversize, faded T-shirt; baggy shorts; white athletic socks—before she pushes the door almost closed and peeps at you from behind it.

Even then all you can think is that she looks *different,* her hair in a ponytail, wisps hanging down around her face. Her lips paler, her face younger.

She does not look pleased.

"Hey," you greet her, suddenly aware you have no reason to be here. "I was on my way home. Thought I'd drop by."

Silence. Heather's face is expressionless; she stares at a point somewhere around the middle of your shirtfront.

"Hang on a sec," she finally says, and the door shuts in your face.

Through the glass panel you see her blurred figure scuttle off to the right, down the hallway. You wait.

And wait.

And wait. The rain picks up again, making a curtain

around the house—but it's okay. You are dry, here on the porch.

When she finally opens the door again, she's wearing denim shorts and a sleeveless blouse, tucked in. Her hair falls over her shoulders, shining and perfect. Her face looks different, too, more defined.

She steps back to let you in. "The rule is," she announces, "call before you come. Then I won't make you wait on the porch."

"I'm sorry. Maybe I shouldn't—"

"No, it's okay. Come in," she urges, when you hesitate. "All I'm saying is, next time call first."

She pulls the door shut behind you. You follow her into the living room, watching her walk. You know you're not the only guy who has watched Heather walk, many, many times through the years. Of course she's got the best rear end anybody's ever seen, anywhere—but she also has a stride that's somewhere between weightless and breathtaking. Her head is always held high.

"I was just doing homework," she says as she leads you into the kitchen. "It's *so* boring. You can give me moral support." The table is covered with books, papers, markers, and index cards. "Sit right here." She points at a chair, starts to slip into the opposite place—then hesitates. "Oh. Did you want something to drink? Although I think all we have right now is Diet Pepsi. Do you like Diet Pepsi?"

"I'm not thirsty. Thanks, though."

"See, if I'd known you were coming, I might have had something else to off—"

"Well, hello!" says a female voice. "I thought I heard the doorbell!"

You turn to see an older version of Heather, in jeans and a black tank top. Blonder. Maybe a little more starched—every curve looks like it's been pushed and padded and smoothed and strapped into place.

Mrs. Mackenzie's eyes are sweeping you up and down. "Aren't you going to introduce us?" she asks Heather, and leans against the doorway.

"This is Austin," says Heather in a flat voice.

"Austin, you are a *doll.* My goodness. You must be over six feet. You left your horse outside, I take it?" It takes you a moment to realize she's referring to your cowboy boots. "Oh, that's not an insult," Mrs. Mackenzie assures you. "I've always been partial to cowboys myself." She straightens, produces a gleaming smile that looks a lot like Heather's. "Would you like a drink, Austin?"

"We've already covered that," Heather says, sounding annoyed. "Don't you have a date, Mother?"

"No, thanks," you tell Mrs. Mackenzie.

"Are you sure? How about a beer?"

"No, ma'am."

"Oh, don't call me that. I'm Linda." Two muffled honks sound from the street; she tosses a glance toward the front of the house. "There's Ronny, right on time. He's very punctual," she adds to you, her nose crinkled. Her eyelashes are very black. "The only thing wrong with him is that he won't come to the door." She steps close to your chair and leans down to advise you in a stage whisper, "Don't *you* do that, when you go to pick up a girl, Austin. Get out of the car and go ring the doorbell. Hear?"

You've got a fine shot of her cleavage. "Yes, ma'am," you say.

Her eyes narrow. She doesn't move. Her breasts look like they're being scooped up and served to you in that black tank top.

"Linda," you add quickly.

"That's better." She stands up. "I'll be back late," she says to Heather, and walks away. Her heeled sandals make a faint *tck-tck-tck* sound on the linoleum and then across the wooden floor in the living room.

Heather frowns into her open book.

The heels pause. The sound of a door opening. "Now, you two don't do anything I wouldn't," Mrs. Mackenzie calls. A couple more *tck*s—the click of the front door shutting—and she's gone.

Heather makes a face. "Whatever. Do you know anything about Shakespeare's sonnets?"

"No. Sorry."

"I've got to write a paper on them. That's what all

these books are. Rough draft's due Monday."

"Maybe I should let you get back to work. I didn't really have any reason—"

"No, no—I'm glad you're here. It beats being alone. I mean," she says, with a quick glance at you, "I don't like to be alone."

"Do you get scared?"

"No." She shuffles through some papers as if looking for something. "I just like to be around people. Some people, anyway."

One of the windows is open a little. You can smell the rain outside. It's afternoon, but dark because of the clouds, and the thunder rumbles like something is coming loose way up in the sky.

When Heather speaks again, her voice is bright. "I know. How about if you recopy my quotations for me? Mrs. Henderson's making me do them over." She hands you some index cards covered with writing and a stack of blank cards. "They're supposed to be in my handwriting, so write *round*." She pushes a pen toward you across the table, then pulls a book closer to her and starts leafing through it.

You don't say anything, just pick up a card and get started . . . very, very slowly. You don't really have any intention of forging her homework. You just want to stay here with her.

Gradually, something inside you relaxes. You don't

have to be entertaining or charming or friendly—just present. You copy a few more words in black ink—writing *round*. But mostly you're just watching Heather, who's bent over one of the books, reading quietly.

Her cheeks look like they've been carved from some fragile stone. Her eyebrows are delicate arcs, her lashes fine-drawn brushes. A lock of hair falls over one cheek; she brushes it back. After a few moments it falls right back again.

Finally, she looks up and catches you watching her.

"You're staring at me," she says. Not flirting, not accusing. Just a statement.

You know what the Pride of the Panthers would say: "You're a lot more interesting than index cards." But you say nothing, and because you don't know what to do if you're not going to flirt, you stop looking at Heather and instead look down at the groove down the center of the table, the space for adding leaves.

"Know what?" you hear Heather say. "I can tell what you're thinking. You don't want to do my note cards for me because you think it's cheating. Only you don't want to say so because you're afraid to be rude. But the thing is, you're wrong; it's not cheating because I did them already. See? But I forgot it's supposed to be in *black* ink. I'd already be through with them if I had anybody but Mrs. Henderson. Most of the other teachers don't even *do* note cards. So you understand, don't you? That it's not cheating?"

You shrug.

"But you're not going to do them anyway, are you?"

"No."

"See, I knew you were going to say that. I could tell by the way you're frowning. Or not exactly frowning. You just have a general frowny attitude about the whole thing. And I don't blame you. I wouldn't want to do somebody else's note cards, either." She sighs and pushes the book away. "And I can't concentrate on some old guy who's been dead a hundred years. Want to listen to CDs?"

Much later, driving home, you realize that you don't remember much of the evening. You don't remember following Heather to the couch in the living room or what music she put on. You don't even remember putting your arm around her. All you remember is her lips touching your face, your neck, your chest; her body pressed against yours through too many layers of clothes, and finally her voice, like bright liquid that joined her hands in pushing you away.

By the time you're home, and in your room alone, all you remember is that when you were sinking, Heather swept you up and pulled you in.

CHAPTER NINE

By the time a few weeks have passed, you're feeling almost like your old self again. It's the easiest thing in the world, being Heather's boyfriend. Like skimming the surface of a lake in a sailboat. All sun and breeze.

If you don't listen to Curtis.

It's Saturday afternoon. You've got a date with Heather tonight, of course. You've spent the last hour listening to some CDs she let you borrow, heavy-beat dance tunes—not your type of music. You're mostly just skimming through them.

As you head toward the refrigerator, Curtis bangs on the back door.

"Brought your mower back," he says, peering at you through the screen. He's got on old bleach-stained shorts, no shirt; his face is streaked with dirt and sweat. "Okay if I grab the keys to the tack room?"

Glancing through the screen door, you see the lawn mower where Curtis pushed it, far across the yard, in front of the shed that once served as an equipment room back in your mother's horse-training days. Now it holds fertilizer and lawn equipment and whatever else shouldn't be left out in the rain. Next to it is the barn, which used to be a stable and now provides shelter for the few calves Becky raises for 4-H.

"Don't worry about the mower," you tell Curtis. "I'll put it up later."

"I'd rather take care of it right now. If my mom looks out and sees it sitting there, I'm going to get the lecture on taking care of other people's possessions. That's one of the long ones."

"'Kay." You shrug. "Help yourself."

"Thanks." The screen squeaks open and Curtis's lean sweaty arm reaches in to snag a key hanging on the peg next to the door.

The screen bangs shut. "Hey," you call. "Go ahead and mow our yard, too. That'll show you can really take care of other people's possessions. Go on—I'll call your mom and tell her how good you did."

Curtis pauses at the bottom of the porch steps, squints up at you. "Sure," he says. "And I'll call your mom and tell her how you're going to come over and paint our front porch."

"How about if we just call it even?"

"Done," says Curtis, and continues on to the tack room.

You dig in the fridge for a Coke, and pull out a Dr Pepper, too, for when Curtis comes back. That's the way it's always been; whenever he drops by he comes in to shoot the breeze. Besides, you're tired of skimming through those CDs. You just don't want to have to look Heather in the eye and admit you didn't bother to listen to them.

You hear Becky coming down the hall, singing one of the songs you just played, one of Heather's songs.

"I ain't invisible, baby, so don't look thro-o-ough me. Our love is possible, baby, so come over to-o-o me." She walks into the kitchen just as you hoist yourself up to sit on the counter to wait for Curtis.

"That's one of those songs that gets stuck in your head," you observe—and it is. A minute ago it was just one of dozens you've heard this afternoon, but now, thanks to Becky, you'll probably be humming it in your sleep tonight.

"I'd rather have that in my head than 'It's a Small World After All.' Or the commercial for Joe Ryan Chevrolet. You want me to sing that for you instead?"

"No," you tell her. "Don't. Please."

Becky grins at you and takes a deep breath—but happens to glance out the window over the sink. She decides not to annoy you; apparently she's been stricken with a sudden desire to straighten the sink area.

First she rinses the plate you left on the counter earlier and places it carefully in the dishwasher. Then she unfolds the dishcloth that sits by the sink, shakes it out, and refolds it. All the time looking out the window toward the tack room.

When Curtis stomps up the back steps, she says real loud, "Is that Curtis Hightower? Quick, lock the refrigerator before he inhales a week's worth of groceries."

Curtis doesn't bother to respond, just steps inside to hang the key to the tack room back up. You don't say anything, either, but hold out the Dr Pepper.

"Thanks." Curtis takes the can from your hand and leans back against the counter by the refrigerator. He pops the top, takes a long drink. Flecks of grass and dirt are stuck to him, mostly on his legs but bits on his arms and chest, too.

Becky makes a big deal out of refolding the dishrag again—carefully, eyes down.

Curtis finally lowers the can and eyes Becky. One corner of his mouth goes up a little. "Hey, Becky. What's this I hear about Robby LeBlanc being madly in love with you?"

Becky's brows start to come together. If it was you, she'd let you have it with both barrels. But with Curtis, all she says is, "He is not."

"Don't tell me you don't like him," Curtis says, deadpan. "I thought for sure you'd want to run your hands through that flowing mane of his."

Becky tries to give him one of those scathing looks she's been practicing lately. The kind that sweeps from head to toe and back again, withering everything in its path. Only this one doesn't make it all the way. It travels up Curtis's legs, loses steam somewhere over his sweaty shorts, and falters completely in the vicinity of his bare chest.

You don't know how Curtis feels about Becky having a crush on him. But he's got to be aware of it; he's not blind. And it's his own fault, for all those years when you ordered Becky to quit following the two of you around, and he'd always feel sorry for her and say, "Aw, let her tag along."

That stupid song is already replaying in your head. *It ain't just physical, baby* . . . something, something.

Becky's face is pink; she won't meet anybody's eyes. Luckily for her the phone rings. She snatches it off the wall. "Oh, hi. Hi, *Aaron,*" she adds, a little too loud. She ducks her head and her hair falls to shield her face.

"Aaron, huh?" Curtis says to you. "Dang, she's going to have to beat these boys off with a stick."

"Nothing much," Becky tells Aaron, but you see her smiling to herself. She heads down the hall slowly, cradling the phone. "Uh-huh. I know." She glances back right before she disappears into her room, but Curtis isn't looking at her anymore.

"So," he's saying to you. "Dobie and I haven't seen

much of you around lately. Been busy with Heather?"

Don't be so cynical, baby . . . da da da da-a-a da. "Yeah. She's all right," you add, just to let Curtis know how things stand.

Curtis doesn't say anything, doesn't nod. After a moment he takes another long drink from his Dr Pepper.

"Listen, if you got to know her, you'd see she's not as bad as you think."

Curtis doesn't look at you, just examines the silver rim of his can.

"It wouldn't kill you to open up your mind a little."

"It's open," he says abruptly. "Open enough to see that she's using you for her senior-year escort."

"She is not."

Curtis shrugs. "Okay. She's not."

That's Curtis. He thinks he's right, so he's not going to argue about it. You ought to keep trying, though. Explain how Heather's not always the same as she is at school. And that even if she is, it's not her fault. She's always been the center of attention—so how could she know what it's like to be treated as if you don't matter? How's she supposed to learn to think about other people if everybody's always thinking about *her*?

Curtis frowns down at his Dr Pepper. "You know, Austy, it doesn't really matter what my opinion is. You're the one going out with her, not me. And whatever happens, I'm not going anywhere. I'll still be around."

He means, if you and Heather split up.

Finally that stupid song gets driven out of your head. Curtis is being ridiculous. Things are just getting started. Things are going great. No way you'd split.

Sometimes you wish Curtis would just keep his mouth shut. Keep his thoughts to himself—Curtis's thoughts are like dark fingers, trying to wrap themselves around your ankles and drag you down.

The truth is, Heather fills all the little bitty gaps you didn't even know you had. Nowadays you're completely different from when—well, you're not even going to think about that. There's nothing to think about. How you used to feel—well, you just don't feel that way anymore, that's all.

You remind yourself how, when Curtis was immersed in Kat, you and Dobie used to tell him to his face that Kat had him pussy whipped. Curtis never got mad, never once got upset about it. Curtis just let the comments rain down around him, brushed them all aside, and went about his business.

That's what you need to do right now. Just brush all his talk about Heather aside. And go on about your business.

One of Becky's calves bawls somewhere in the field behind the barn. The old screen on the kitchen door vibrates in the grip of an unseen breeze. It's a bright, sunny day outside. A beautiful day. You can smell the fresh-cut grass.

"Hey, guess what?" Curtis says out of the blue. "I actually spoke to the old man on the phone."

"What'd he want?" you ask. You don't have to ask who "the old man" is. Even though Mr. Hightower eventually married Tiffani-with-an-*i*, Curtis still hasn't gotten around to forgiving him for being unable to keep his pants zipped in the first place.

"Get this. He asked me if I wanted to go skiing over Christmas with him and What'sherface."

"What'd you say?" you ask, although you already know. Curtis has never gone to visit his dad in Nevada. Won't get on the plane, won't get in the car to go to the airport. He'll barely even talk to his dad on the phone.

"I told him, 'Sorry, I got things to do.' "

"Gave up a free ski trip?"

Curtis shrugs, takes another sip of Dr Pepper.

"Might not be so bad," you point out. "The skiing part might make up for the rest of it."

Curtis just shakes his head. He's never understood what an opportunity he's dismissing with his dad. He just doesn't get that he has a chance some people will never have.

"When he was here he never came to a single one of my games. Now all of a sudden he's asking what position I play. So I just tell him I've got to go, that's all. Tell him I've got stuff to do—which is true. And he always says, how about if I call back later? And I always say, sure, do that. But somehow I'm always busy, when later rolls around. And mostly, so is he."

"But he did call in the first place," you tell him.

Curtis shrugs again. "He made his choice. I've moved on from there."

That's the way Curtis is; everything tallied and weighed, and while he turns his back on whatever he decides isn't worth his while, he also digs his heels in on whatever he cares about. Nothing you ever say can change that—one way or the other.

"Thanks for the DP." Curtis tosses his empty can into the bin. "I've got to go get cleaned up. Dobie and me and Stargill are going to a movie in Burlington. I guess you probably already got plans?"

"Yeah. What're you going to see?"

"*Mayhem.*"

"Which one's that?"

"The one where a bunch of terrorists take over the Pentagon. It's supposed to be good," Curtis adds. "You're welcome to ditch Heather and come along."

"Maybe some other time."

Curtis just nods—that's what he expected. "Later, then," he says, unconcerned, and heads out the door.

The screen bangs shut. You hop off the counter and head back into your room, taking the half-finished Coke with you.

Da da—da da da da. "Don't be so cynical, baby," you sing under your breath, and turn up the volume.

Used to be you'd hang around practice to give Dobie a ride home. You'd wait for him to finish straightening the locker room, and then drive along in the truck listening to him talk about whatever was on his mind that day— usually food or girls, and in that order.

Nowadays, Curtis is the one who takes Dobie home. Nowadays you spend more time with Heather than with your friends.

Can't wait for practice to be over, because most days she waits for you. Sometimes you go to the Dairy Queen, where Heather orders a Diet Coke while you get a jumbo ice water or a Sprite. Sometimes you even order fries because it seems like you're hungry more often these days.

Whenever you take Heather home, she doesn't move to get out when you pull up in front of the house.

Sometimes you make out with her, but a lot of times you just sit and listen to her talk. You like the way her voice sounds, like music that doesn't have anything to do with anything.

It's as if you've been treading water furiously, and now you can stretch your foot out and just barely touch bottom.

One night after a game, you and Curtis and Dobie come out of the field house, and there she is, standing in that same circle of her friends under the streetlight. Your pickup stands alone a few yards off, where the light starts to fade away.

"Hi!" Heather says, coming to meet you. Curtis gives her a stiff nod, which is as friendly as he can ever get to someone he doesn't like. She doesn't return it. "Excuse me, my face is up *here,*" she's saying to Dobie.

Dobie's eyes flick quickly away from Heather's breasts, his face turning dark with embarrassment. He pulls his cowboy hat down over his eyes.

"And on that note," Curtis says, "I guess we'll be heading on out. See you tomorrow, Austy," he says, moving toward his own car a few rows over.

"Great game," you call after him.

Heather follows you around to the passenger side of the pickup. "I'm sorry," she says as you open the door, "but I couldn't take being leered at by Hopalong Toothpick. And I hope you don't mind if I don't want to pal around with Curtis. It's not that I don't *like* him," she adds, sliding into her seat. "He's really cute and all. But this is senior year, and it's like, do I want to hang out with King Tightass when this is the primo party year of my life? I think *not*!"

"He's my best friend," you point out, and shut the door a little harder than necessary. When you walk around to the other side, you can feel how you've stiffened up—a lot more than when Curtis said he thought Heather was using you. That's different, somehow, from Heather telling you she doesn't want to be around a guy who's been like a brother ever since your mothers put the two of you in the same playpen.

"He's so irritating," Heather says when you get in. "He always acts like I'm such a bimbo. You know he blames me, don't you? Just because his little girlfriend told him off at my party last year. Like it was my fault she got puke drunk."

"I don't think he even remembers—"

"I'm hot," Heather interrupts. "Could you turn on the air?"

It's not really that hot; not since the sun went down. You think it'd be a good evening to drive with the windows down, to let the warm grass smells wash around you. You don't like the way she makes you feel about your best friend.

But you roll up the window and obey.

As soon as you start the engine, Heather twists the rearview mirror around and peers into it, fluffing and picking at her bangs. "Curtis needs to stop acting like he's so virtuous. Everybody knows he and Kat broke up because she didn't want to have sex, and he did."

"I don't think that's what happened."

"That's what I heard, and I believe it."

There is a story about Curtis—the story about him crying in the tack room when his dad ran off with Tiffani-with-an-*i*—that might make Heather see him in a different light. It's why Curtis takes sex so seriously, even now, even though he's about to turn eighteen. It's why Kat was the only one he ever did it with; he was crazy in love with her.

Problem is, you can't tell the story. For one thing, it's not yours to tell.

What "everybody knows" is partly true. It's true that after a few weeks of "doing it" Kat wanted to back the whole relationship up, while Curtis—having gotten used to enjoying all the benefits—wanted to keep things the way they were. By the time Curtis was ready to agree, Kat was off on a "if-you'd-really-loved-me" jag, and it was too late.

You didn't see that it was anything to break up over. In your opinion, Kat might just as well have asked him to give back her lost virginity. Kat was lucky to have Curtis in the first place. She could have gotten any of the hundred other guys you know who *don't* see sex as the first step on the road to matrimony, three kids, and a Suburban.

But you can't tell Heather any of this. She wouldn't understand; she's a girl, and besides, it's obvious she doesn't care to see it any way but hers.

Heather stops picking at her bangs and pulls her purse up off the floorboard. You reach for the mirror to adjust it so you can back out.

"Wait a minute." She digs in the purse, pulls out a small brush, and starts fluffing again.

So you shut the engine off and roll down your window again.

Then you sigh.

"It's just so humid," Heather says, as if that explains something.

You lean back against the headrest and try to get interested in watching Heather and her hair. She must feel you looking at her, because she glances at you. You don't bother to give her a smile, and she examines you for a moment before returning her gaze to the mirror.

She starts fishing in her purse again. Her hands make a scrabbling, shuffling noise as they search and dig for some mysterious girl thing.

This—waiting for hair to be brushed—is the price of dating Heather. This, and avoiding your best friend.

"Now, don't be mad." Heather snaps her purse shut,

drops it onto the floorboard. She slides over, tucks her arm into yours. "It just kills me when you get all frowny and quiet. It's like, God, I'm going to be the first person in the history of the world that Austin Reid doesn't like. I'd die." She lays her head on your shoulder. She's light against your arm, and she's not wearing any perfume tonight; there's only the faint scent of her shampoo or lotion—something clean and sweet.

"I know I'm a snob," you hear her say. "That's why I'm counting on you to be a good influence."

Well, it's not like you aren't used to being around people with strong opinions. One thing Heather and Curtis have in common is that they're both opinionated. Honest, too.

The only real difference between them, you think, is that Heather's thoughts seem to fall out of her mouth without much presorting. That's all Curtis does, is sort.

It feels awkward, just sitting there. So your arm goes around her—you try not to be stiff about it. She nestles into you; her class ring flashes in the dim light as she rests her hand on your thigh. You figure you ought to say something but don't know what.

Both of you sit there without a word; people walk by in the parking lot; their voices come and go while the warmth of Heather's hand seeps through your jeans.

"Don't be mad," she says again, softly—she's very still, her head on your chest so that you can't see her face.

You don't say anything. You're not mad, really—not anymore. Just deflated.

It's a slow infusion of electricity when her hand begins to move. "I don't like you to be angry with me," she says, and her hand's sliding deliberately up your thigh.

It disappears under your shirttail.

"What are you doing?" you ask, though her knuckles are warm against your belly, tugging your pants open. The air in the truck is so still all of a sudden that you can hardly breathe.

Her voice is muffled against your chest. "If you want me to stop, just say so."

You're no fool; you don't say so. Her hand gets busy; your breath gets ragged. It doesn't take long before your body breaks into one of those tiny uncontrolled shudders, and you hear a low, pleased laugh from Heather. That's when you try to get her to look up so you can kiss her quick and drive to someplace private—but she pulls away.

And lowers her head to your lap.

There are two worlds: One, outside the open window, people walking by, laughing, talking, coming perilously close to the pickup—which, thankfully, is high off the ground—while you struggle to look straight ahead and keep your face empty of expression. Like a guy who's just sitting there, bored.

The other world is inside the cab of the pickup; soft sounds and the feel of Heather's hair moving back and forth like silk under your hand, and the strained quiver you finally give, trying not to move or cry out.

You're still dazed when she sits up and peers into your face. "Did you like that?"

"Yes." Your voice is thick. You pull your jeans back together, a little embarrassed because she seems so matter-of-fact, while for you this was quite an amazing thing.

"Did you know your eyes go out of focus when I touch you down there?" she asks, smoothing her hair as she settles back into her seat. "You forget to be all mad and serious. I like that. I like making Mr. Good Influence lose control."

Okay, so she's not a tease. She just likes things to be her idea.

Which is okay with you; turns out she's got some pretty good ideas. It's only a few weeks after that when the two of you end up parked out behind the old Methodist church, at the end of a dirt road under a tree. And before that evening's done you've gotten down to business with Heather Mackenzie unbuttoned, unhooked, unzipped, and underneath you on the seat of your own pickup.

Yep, Heather's ideas scatter bad feelings the way a puff of air scatters dust.

CHAPTER ELEVEN

Sixth game. Final score: Panthers, 21; Bulldogs, 10.

On the way home, everybody is hollering, hanging out the bus windows, messing around like this is some crazed field trip. You're right there with them, waving and yelling at every car that passes.

Well, almost everybody. In the seat ahead of you, Curtis sits stiff and silent. He won't turn around, won't talk to anybody, even though the game is over and he doesn't need to concentrate anymore.

You don't have to talk to him to know why he's so quiet. Curtis screwed up tonight. Blew man-to-man coverage on third and ten. He didn't slip or trip or get outrun. He simply had his head up his ass for a change and was nowhere near the guy he was supposed to be covering.

The bus must be close to halfway home and he still hasn't said a word.

You lean forward over the seat. "We won," you remind Curtis, right in his ear.

Curtis doesn't even turn his head. He's probably doing his own visualizing now, watching himself over and over, seeing himself realize that the guy streaking toward the end zone is *his* guy.

He's always like this. There are two things that really bother Curtis; one is not having Kat. The other one is screwing up in football.

Tonight, his screwup kept a Bulldog drive alive. In Curtis's book, that means he hand delivered them a touchdown.

"Listen," you tell the back of his head. "Forget it. Coach'll remind you quick enough."

A car honks outside. This one has purple-and-white crepe paper streaming from the antenna; Go Panthers is written on the windows in shoe polish. Everybody else on the left side of the bus is cheering out the windows.

"Go get drunk with Dobie," you try, feeling bad for not offering to dump Heather for the evening—even though you know Curtis always goes straight home after a bad game. Specifically, after *he* has a bad game.

When he still doesn't say anything, you give up. Let him act like that, if he wants. He doesn't need any help from you, anyway.

You know what'll happen. He'll mope around all evening. It'll take him the rest of the night to get things back in perspective. In the end, he'll remind himself to be more alert next time. And in the morning, he'll be calm and cool and ready to face those game films. The game films won't be able to tell Curtis anything he doesn't already know.

You lean out the window again, feeling the wind lift the still-sweaty hair from your scalp. With the kind of mood Curtis is in right now, it's actually a mercy that he's going straight home. Being around Curtis would be even worse than sitting home alone.

You didn't screw up tonight. Well, you did drop a couple of catches, but still it was you personally who put two-thirds of the points on the board. You've got no reason to feel bad, not next to Curtis.

And shoot, even if you did have a reason for feeling bad—which you don't—you'd never act like it. You'd take that reason for feeling bad, and stick it in the back of your mind. You'd shove it down inside and keep your mouth shut and lie low until everybody else forgot what happened.

You keep your head and one arm out the window, letting the wind plug your ears. You shut your eyes and feel the air rushing by, feel the bus wheels whine under you. The great thing about handling mistakes *your* way is that after awhile your screwups and hurts don't matter anymore.

Down deep inside you there's a big old pile of things that everybody but you has forgotten.

•   •   •

At the field house, whoops and yells and laughter are billowing around you.

"Way to *be*," somebody says; a hand pounds your shoulder, so you figure whoever it is must be talking to you.

"Thanks," you say, not bothering to look around. Curtis came in, grabbed his clothes, and left; he'll change at home.

"Great game, Reid," somebody says.

You don't bother to say thanks this time. You just nod and bend to tie your shoe.

"Hey, Austin. You going out?"

It's Dobie, coming around the corner of the lockers with a wet mop braced on his shoulder.

"Yeah," you answer.

Dobie slops the mop onto the floor where Stargill was squirting Gatorade all over the place. He swirls the mop around, painting huge wet circles. "Want to come with me and Jason and Brett? We're going to get some beer."

"Sorry, can't make it," you say.

"C'mon, Austin. It'll be fun. We might rent some videos. You know," he says, leaning forward to whisper. "*Videos*."

"No, thanks."

Dobie shakes his head. "I always thought Curtis was bad when he was going out with Kat," he says, giving the mop an extra flourish, "but Heather has flat out busted your balls."

"Shut up," you snap at him.

The mop stops. A moment later it starts moving again, but not leisurely like before. Now it's a quick back-and-forth. When you glance over, you see one spot of red flaming Dobie's cheek like somebody slapped him.

Of course—he was kidding, the way the two of you always kidded Curtis. You were supposed to kid back.

If Curtis was here—and not sitting around like a gargoyle—he'd say, *What's got into you?*

"Sorry, Dobe," you tell him, ashamed.

Dobie nods once, quickly, his eyes on his work. When he's done he picks up the mop, shoulders it, and scurries off without looking back.

You turn back to your locker. You said you're sorry—what else can you do?

Nothing, tonight. Because Heather's waiting.

CHAPTER TWELVE

In the field house Monday afternoon, Dobie seems okay. He nods and says hi. He doesn't ask how your date went, or start chattering about his weekend like he sometimes does. But then, he's pretty busy with his duties.

Coach calls for full pads. He says he's going out to the field, and everybody'd better be with him in five minutes. "Move it, girls," he says on his way out the door. "I'm not in the mood to baby-sit."

Curtis has to know what's coming. It doesn't seem to bother him, though; he asks how it went with Heather Friday night. You say fine. The two of you finish dressing out.

What's coming doesn't bother him, but it bothers you. It shouldn't—God knows you've done your share of hammering other guys during Bull-in-a-Ring. But it does bother you; just a little, that's all. Like gum on the bottom of your shoe, that you can't quite scrape off. Because there's no point in doing this—Curtis doesn't need to be pounded into the ground for a mistake he's already suffered over, fought through, and won. Not Curtis, who thinks of football as a higher form of art.

Probably that's why your chest is a little tight. Even though you know this drill isn't any big deal. No big deal, not really. And it's probably why you can't quite bring yourself to look at Curtis.

"Go ahead," you tell him, bending to tie your shoe on the bench in front of the locker. "I'll be out in a second."

"You okay?" Curtis asks. As if it's you who's about to get gored and trampled.

"Yeah." Your face feels like it's turning to stone. Curtis goes on outside. When you pull the shoelace, intending to tighten it, your hands jerk so hard that it snaps in two.

By the time you find a new lace, get it into your cleats and head out to the field, warm-ups are almost over. You just have time to do a few quick stretches, because Coach is telling everybody to form the ring.

"On account of forgetting who he was supposed to cover," he announces. "Hightower gets the weekly Head up His Ass Award."

Brett Stargill's standing across from you, feet planted like tree trunks, a faint smile flickering like sunlight over his face. Your own face feels so stiff it could shatter. You lift your dangling chin strap, snap it into place.

Curtis steps into the center without a word.

"Everybody down," Coach commands.

"Set." Across the ring, Stargill hunkers down at the same time you do; he's your mirror image.

Coach blows his whistle at the same instant he points to Jason Cox. Immediately, Cox blasts off his stance, straight into Curtis. But Curtis is crouched and ready, and when they meet, he actually drives Cox back a step or two.

For some reason you're remembering something you haven't thought about in years; you and Curtis, ten years old, sneaking one of Curtis's dad's cigars out to the trees beyond the stock tank. Feeling hard-edged and bold, trading puffs—till you noticed Curtis's face was kind of green, and then you couldn't deny the fact you were getting pretty sick yourself.

Cox trots back into the circle, into the wrong place. Coach already has his whistle back in his mouth.

Tweeet! He points to Shea, who takes his shot. He and Curtis come together like two rams, and the impact forces Curtis back almost to the other side. Shea's quicker than Cox at getting back into the circle.

You're remembering how you and Curtis laid there till the world stopped spinning, then tottered weakly back over to Curtis's house, side by side, swearing a solemn vow never to touch tobacco again.

Tweeet! Thomas's turn.

And when you walked inside, Curtis's mom was looking out the kitchen window saying *"Is that smoke out there?"* And sure enough a spark had caught in the dried-up late summer grass. The Parkersville Volunteer Fire Department came, which was exciting, and a deputy from the county sheriff, which wasn't, because you threw up all over his boots and he threatened to arrest you.

Tweeet! Ragsdale.

Curtis is still standing. He's the one who told you they don't arrest kids for throwing up. You already knew it, but you were still scared, till Curtis said it out loud—and that made it true.

Tweeet! Coach's finger points to you.

You explode.

The next thing you know, Curtis is lying on his back with you on top of him. You don't look at his face, just get up quickly; Curtis is slower, but Coach is already blowing his whistle again and then suddenly Curtis is down again, this time hit from behind by Brett Stargill. When he gets up he's a little unsteady, with a clot of turf stuck in his face mask.

Coach calls them on from the front, from the sides, from behind, where Curtis can't see it coming.

And then it doesn't matter because Coach is calling them on so fast that Curtis barely has time to get to his feet, much less look around.

When Coach finally gives it an extra-long now-we're-done blow, Curtis lies there and doesn't get up right away.

"Everybody line up for wind sprints," Coach hollers.

You're frozen, staring down at your best friend curled up on the ground like a dead shrimp.

"Reid! You deaf? Line up for wind sprints."

So you do what you have to do; you shove down whatever it is you're feeling and walk away; you watch yourself walk away and get in line with everybody else.

When you look back to check, Curtis is wincing as he gets to his feet. He doesn't mind, he knows it's just business. But still, it might take awhile to shove this one down—the fact that you let Curtis get up from Bull-in-a-Ring without any help.

CHAPTER THIRTEEN

It's a comfort to watch Heather get dressed.

Mrs. Mackenzie is out with Ronny. What's left of the afternoon is leaking away and you're just lying on Heather's bed, wide awake, eyes open, because getting up is as impossible as floating off the ground.

She's already got her panties on—that breath catching little scrap of silk. You love the way she pulls the front of her bra together, love the way her breasts seem to expand, as if pushed in and up by unseen hands.

She snaps the bra closed, reaches for her blouse . . . and sees you watching.

She tosses the blouse aside and turns toward the mirror. A quick glance at you again before she focuses on her own reflection, as if she's forgotten you're there.

She hasn't. You know by now: It's a comfort to Heather to let you watch her get dressed.

Looking at her, at that beautiful face and all those breathtaking ins and outs, you can admit the truth—you don't really care about anything else. Don't particularly care about your friends, your family, school. Even Bull-in-a-Ring is a distant memory, because now you are here.

The mattress cradles you like a cocoon. You'd like just to lie here, flatter and flatter, and never have to leave this place.

"You know something?" Heather winds one lock of hair slowly around her finger. "You're the first guy I've let in my room. I never let guys in. Never." When she lets the lock of hair fall, it brushes her skin just above the champagne-colored lace.

"One time," she continues, staring into her own eyes—Heather can get as caught up in her reflection as you can in the real thing—"Brad Echols came around throwing pebbles at my window, trying to get me to let him in. But I wouldn't. That's silly, isn't it?" She turns her head a little to one side, checking her face from a slightly different angle. "I mean, not letting guys in. Because my room is a lot safer than the couch if Mom comes back all of a sudden. It's not like, roll off the couch and get dressed right away—can you say high school? There's always a scene if Mom even thinks I've done something, the hypocrite."

Always? you think, and wonder—not for the first time—how many guys she's been with. But you don't want to ask, because then she might ask you the same about your exes.

Instead you watch the way her hair slides and swings over her shoulder blades. "Want to hear something funny?" Heather says, and goes on without waiting for an answer. "The first guy I dated—he was a real jerk. An older guy—he was seventeen, and I was thirteen. I only ever did it with him in the first place because I was scared I'd lose him if I didn't. But then after we did do it, I was still scared that he'd get bored. So I was like this doormat, letting him do whatever he wanted. Can you imagine me being a doormat?" Again, she doesn't wait for an answer. "Every single time I'd just end up underneath him and he'd just keep going until he was finished. And I'd be left with nothing but this awful, empty feeling, and sticky underwear for the rest of the night. So I finally got up the guts to dump him. And guess what he did?"

"I don't know."

"He cried. Can you believe it?"

She laughs. Something in her voice chills you a little. You pull the sheet up higher over your chest.

You don't know what you'll say if she asks you about your first time. It actually was a lot like Heather described, except you didn't "keep going." It was over so quick you barely even *got* going. It happened during a commercial break while you and the girl were at her house watching TV. Of course, you'd been kissing and touching each other for a long time, but the main event was finished so quickly you didn't even miss any of *Saturday Night Live*.

Heather doesn't ask you anything. She turns away from the mirror, bends to pick up her blouse from the floor. "Blech! Makeup stain." She drops the blouse and gives you a mock glare. "Why didn't you tell me?"

"I didn't see it."

She's walking over to the closet. "That's why everybody likes you—you never see anything wrong with anybody." She starts rifling through the clothes, looking for something to wear. "Hey. Recognize this?" She reaches into the closet, pulls out a plaid skirt on a hanger. Short, of course. "Don't you remember?"

You shake your head.

"I wore it That Night."

"What night?"

"You know." She waits, then when you still have no clue: "The night of Our First Time."

Oh. "It was dark," you explain. "I couldn't see much."

Heather looks annoyed. She hangs the skirt back in the closet, slides a bunch of hangers over to bury it.

The hangers make a screeching noise as she moves them across one by one; solids, prints, pastels, plaid, lace.

Then she stops and pushes the other clothes aside to look at a dress. She slides her hand down the silky fabric. You don't recognize that one, either.

Heather sighs. Obviously, this dress has a nice memory

attached to it. "Am I supposed to remember that one, too?" you ask.

"No," she says, and sweeps the dress aside. "You know what I like about you? The way you smell. Some guys slap on cologne like it's mosquito repellent. But you just smell like a person. Like sun and wind. Maybe just a little sweat. And I like the way in the evenings sometimes you get a little five o'clock shadow, like you need a shave. It gives you this bad-boy look. Very sexy."

She pulls out a blouse, removes it from the hanger, starts to put it on—then glances at you, and with the faintest of smiles, drapes the blouse over the doorknob before she walks back over to the mirror, and begins brushing her hair. The show's not over yet.

She scoops her hair up with both hands, holding it on top of her head in a mass of curls. Her neck is long and arched. "If you look in that bottom right-hand drawer, there's a basket with ribbons and stuff. Can you dig through and find a clip that looks like a butterfly? It's gold, with big wings."

You roll over, reach down, and pull the drawer open. There's a bunch of papers in it, and a box made of dark wood, with a duck inlaid on the lid; it looks like something that a man would own. But it's the only thing that's even remotely like a basket, so you take the lid off.

The box is empty except for a piece of paper that's

been torn to bits and taped back together. It's old; the Scotch tape that holds it together is yellowing.

it's better this way i know Heather will forget i hope you will forgive

"Not that drawer." Heather's beside you suddenly, slamming the drawer shut so quickly that it almost catches your fingers. "I said the *right* side."

"Sorry," you say.

"Forget it." Scowling, she goes back to stand in front of the mirror and starts playing with her hair again, but her hands can't seem to remember where they left off; locks slide from beneath her fingers and fall down her neck while she frowns at her own reflection.

"I didn't mean—"

"I said *forget it.* Are you deaf?"

"No," you say, getting angry, too. You roll onto your back again. "I'm not."

"Apparently"—Heather whirls away from the mirror—"you are." She walks over to the blouse hanging on the doorknob, pulls it free, jerks it over her head. Snatches her jeans up off the floor where she left them.

She won't come sit on the bed to put her jeans on but turns her back to you, teetering to balance on one foot while she thrusts the other one into the pants leg.

119

She's pretty angry. You think about the note, all torn up, then taped back together. About how it looks kind of old, and how she doesn't want anybody to see it. And how it seems to be a good-bye.

And suddenly you think you understand why she's so upset. "Heather . . . " You pull a pillow onto your chest. Push it off again; you're still thinking. Roll onto your side, prop up one elbow. "It's okay to—if you ever wanted to talk about your dad, you could talk to me."

She still refuses to face you; you hear her zip the jeans. "You don't talk about *your* dad." Her voice is cold.

"There's nothing to talk about."

"There's nothing for me to talk about, either."

"But I don't remember anything," you begin—and stop. Because there is the one thing you remember.

Heather stalks over, pulls open the bottom right-hand drawer, which, sure enough, is brimming with ribbons and barrettes. She picks out the butterfly clip. Steps over to the mirror and starts brushing her hair again. Briskly, this time, pulling the brush through so fast it crackles.

"You do remember something," she says, twisting her hair up behind her head. "I can tell. So go ahead. Spill it."

She holds the twist with one hand, slides the butterfly clip in. *Snap!* It's done. Perfectly.

You don't particularly want to spill it. But you feel like reaching out a little, and you do want her to trust you—although you don't really expect it to be quick and easy. She's so touchy about things.

So you'll put your own self on the line first. "Well, there is this one thing," you tell her. You feel your face get a little warm and pull the pillow close to your chest again. "But it's more like a feeling or a dream. Only it was real."

"Go ahead."

You finger the corner of the pillowcase, trying to think what to say. You don't really want to say anything, but somebody has to go first. "I must have been very little—I remember sitting up on the bathroom counter next to him, and we'd shave together. Except I was playing, you know—I had this toy razor. Not a real one."

She doesn't say anything. Just turns her head this way and that, checking her twist for flaws.

"That's all," you tell her, and roll back on the bed.

"Rats," says Heather. Apparently she's found a flaw—she pulls the clip out. "Your dad died from cancer, right?" she asks, picking up the brush to start all over again.

"Yeah."

"So everybody knew ahead of time that he was going to, you know. Die." She brushes her hair out with businesslike strokes. "I'll bet you got to go say good-bye to him and everything. Didn't you?"

"I don't know."

"I'm sure you did. It's very important. It's like something's unfinished, if you don't get to do it." She pulls the hair up into that same smooth, shining twist, clips it with a *snap!* "I used to have dreams where I said good-bye. But I don't need anybody's pity," she adds, giving you a defiant glance in the mirror.

"I don't think anybody pities you."

"That's right. They don't." She checks her hair—it's identical to the way she did it a second ago, as far as you can tell. "This looks okay, doesn't it?"

"It looks great. Was that note from your dad?" you ask.

Heather freezes, blinks at her reflection for a moment. Then, without a word, she walks away. "You know what's good about jeans?" she asks, keeping her back to you as she scoops up the makeup-stained blouse. "Blue is actually a neutral color. Anything goes with them. I'll bet you didn't know that." She pauses there, blouse in hand, as if she's suddenly lost track of what she's doing. You see her take a deep breath. "Did you ever have this feeling like you're not sad or anything, but like something's squeezing the back of your eyes? Like you want to cry, but can't?"

She's just standing there in the middle of the room, and you notice for the first time how thin her shoulders are. She's always seemed so much bigger than life—but at this moment, when she's not posing or smiling or bossing people around, she actually looks quite small.

"Yeah," you tell her. "I know what you mean." You want to add something else—only you don't know what.

Comfort her in some way, maybe—only you don't know how. Get up? Walk all the way over there and hug her?

"You've been here a long time," she says, and when she turns to look at you her eyes are clear and blank, like a doll's eyes. "You'd better be going home."

She means it.

She busies herself as you get dressed; she tidies up the dresser, straightens the chair, without a word she hands you one of your shoes that somehow ended up behind the closet door.

On the front porch, she seems almost fragile—maybe because her makeup's mostly worn off, which makes her look a lot younger. You give her a good-bye kiss. She puts up with it at first, then pulls away the way a little kid pulls away from putting medicine on a stinging scrape. You'd like to tell her that anytime she wants to talk, you'll be there—but she's already going inside.

She's shut the door before you even step off the porch.

CHAPTER FOURTEEN

You keep thinking about her all the way home, all through the evening. There is definitely a tender little edge of hurt peeking out from underneath Heather's shining exterior. You've always known it's there, somewhere way underneath. You recognize it because you've got one, yourself.

Heather doesn't wait for you after practice the next day. And when you call her in the evening, her phone rings and rings until you realize she's either not home or she turned it off.

Around nine-thirty she finally answers. Mom's heading off to bed; she gives you the evil eye to remind you to keep it down and not stay up too late.

You take the cordless and hole up in your room. "Hi, it's me," you begin, real low—but Heather slaps you right away with brightness and chatter, acting like nothing unusual happened yesterday.

She hardly even pauses for breath: She just got home from shopping with Melissa—a new Contempo opened up in Fort Worth, which she doesn't expect you to be excited about, but you should be, and they had the soft opening this week before the grand opening on Saturday, and she and Melissa were finally able to get some *real* clothes.

She describes what *real* clothes are. You wait for a chance to talk about something more important—exactly what, you have no idea. You figure it'll come to you when Heather lets up. She'll have to let up in a minute; nobody could keep this up for long.

Heather can. Just when she seems to be running out of steam, she says she hasn't finished her homework; she's got to go; sorry to keep you up late, see you tomorrow!

And then the dial tone is buzzing in your ear.

That night you toss and turn. Not like those nights when you used to wake and lie there with your mind crusted over by a dull wish that everything would just go blank—no, this is sleeplessness with a purpose. Something about you and Heather is lacking, it's missing a connection. It's missing *something,* only you don't know what to do about it.

You keep thinking about her description of her first time. One more item in the long list of things you fail at is that, quite often, you "just keep going" with Heather. She's never seemed to mind—in fact, she's always encouraged it—but now you see that she's done everything for your benefit, sexually; Heather gives, gives, gives—and you've been eager to receive, receive, receive.

Next opportunity, you decide, you're going to do more for her. You're going to take your own sweet time with Heather Mackenzie. You won't hurry or rush the count. You'll tease her the way she always teases you—till Heather's the one who forgets everything but being touched.

Here's the play: You'll start out with kissing that will gradually move lower and blur into touching, and you'll listen to her breathing—or the way she holds her breath—that, and the tension of her body will tell you what she likes best.

You decide to run the play on Friday after school because that allows plenty of time—no practice today, and no game tonight because this week is one of two in the season with a Saturday game.

So you take her for a Coke at the Dairy Queen, then home, where you start all the action outside on the front porch, not even trying to get inside her clothes—not yet. Keep both hands firm on her back. Do not stick your tongue in her ear. Not yet. She's teasing you a little, nibbling on your lips before going for the deep kiss.

When your hands slide down to her rear, she rubs you through your jeans, and at the catch in your breath she gives that low laugh and presses closer. But when your own hands move out of her neutral zone, she puts both her hands on your shoulders to push you away.

You can almost feel her thinking. She enjoys taking you to the edge—and occasionally over—in places where you can't—or shouldn't—react. Right now she's got you upright, standing on concrete, outdoors, in plain view of the street. There's no reason to push you away.

So she doesn't.

You take your time, and after awhile longer your hands are spending time in places they've more or less passed over before, zeroing in here and there, and after awhile she's trying to press herself up against your fingers, trying to get you to stop somewhere and focus. She's forgetting to kiss you back and her hands have forgotten what they're doing, and then she's forgetting to breathe—she's clinging to you, and when air comes bursting out of her in a shaky sigh, you hear yourself give a low laugh that sounds familiar.

She hears it. Her whole body grows stiff. She puts her palms against your shoulders and *shoves,* so hard you have to step back to keep your balance.

She's upset. And now you have to fight against a vacuum that wants to suck your body onto hers; your whole body is leaning forward, wanting to tackle her, drive her down onto the concrete porch and peel her jeans off and do what needs to be done.

Something's wrong. But you have no idea what it is. It's not like you've never touched her before. And you did not imagine the way she was clinging to you. You did not imagine that little explosion of her breath against your neck.

You will burst, if this is it.

She fumbles in her purse for her keys with one hand, and with the other makes a swiping gesture at her mouth.

As if she's trying to wipe off your touch.

"Is something wrong?" It can't be—she's got to be about to burst, too. You know she has.

"You think I'm going to fall at your feet," she tosses the words over her shoulder as her keys blunder, jangling around the lock. "You paw me a few times, and I'm supposed to beg you to *do it* to me. Like you're *so* irresistible," she adds, and gives you a disgusted glance. "You're just some clumsy little high school boy. Except you drive a *pickup*. Which makes you a clumsy little *hick*."

She's like a nail gun, driving words in; it hurts to breathe all of a sudden. You take a step back.

"That's right, get out of here." She gives the uncooperative key ring a vicious shake. "Damn it! I can't find the right key!"

You're already turning away, moving down the sidewalk in slow motion—it's like wallowing through thick

128

mud, and you can't walk away fast enough.

"Just remember, you were the one panting for it. Not me." She hurls the words at your back as you step off the curb. "Not me," Heather says again, and it sounds like somebody is strangling her.

CHAPTER FIFTEEN

The air has caved in on top of you.

Her perfume is wrapped tight around you like a cocoon, it's woven into your shirt, laced over your skin, and your foot presses harder and harder on the gas until by the end of the block you're going too fast to brake for the stop sign.

No one hears the squeal of rubber on asphalt as you take the corner. No one sees. No one follows.

You are all the things you've ever failed at, sitting on top of a couple tons of steel zigzagging in and out of traffic. If there is any justice, this pickup will get crushed like an empty Coke can.

But it doesn't, and you end up at home, pulling up the gravel driveway to the back of the house. Mom's car isn't here; she must still be at work.

You turn off the engine. Get out of the truck. Shut

the driver's side door and lean back against it. Take one deep breath. And another.

And another.

Your arms are folded; you unfold them and they fall immediately to your sides. The keys drop with a jangle into the gravel. Wind plays in the treetops along the fence. You just stand there letting the truck hold you up.

Far across the yard at the Hightowers' house, a screen door screeches, then slams. Like some sick animal crawling out of sight, you start moving blindly toward your home.

You've dropped your keys somewhere, don't know where. Becky's rubber boots aren't in their place on the porch; she must be out in the barn feeding her calves. That means the back door is unlocked, so you walk in, head through the kitchen. Go down the hall, past the doorway of your room, which is still and silent, and dark like a cave. Your arms are dangling at your sides, your heart is beating in uneven little scratches at the inside of your chest.

You thought everything was okay. You thought you were okay.

Wrong—it took only one slight shift to break you into pieces.

Your feet carry you into the bathroom. When they stop, you are stranded in front of the sink. You don't bother to look at the reflection. You know what he looks like, eyes flat and muddy. Everything twisted.

"Oh, God," you hear the guy in the mirror whisper. He sounds like he's being squeezed.

You wait for the squeezed feeling to pass. It holds firm, coiled around you like a python. You'd like to slide down to the floor, lay your head down on the white tile and just quit feeling, totally. You don't ever want to feel anything again.

So you lock the bathroom door. Watch your own hand open the medicine cabinet. And take out the box holding your dad's razor.

The house is quiet. In the refrigerator, the ice maker kicks on with a lurch. You can even hear the faint trickle of water along the copper tubing—it scrapes you as if you're one long raw nerve.

You open the wooden box. The golden razor lies in state on red velvet. It is telling you to wind down, come to an end.

If you pick up the razor, all you have to do is twist the end to open up the head. And then you can extract the blade.

Somewhere far off, a phone rings. It rasps away into the silence while you notice how translucent the skin over your wrist is, and how, close up, it's infinitesimally wrinkled, like you're a ninety-year-old man. The veins are buried blue but not so deep.

It wouldn't surprise you if you didn't bleed at all, if

you were dry inside. If you didn't feel a thing.

"Austy!" Becky bellows.

The phone has stopped ringing. You're floating somewhere between intention and reality.

Socked feet pad down the hall. "Phone," Becky calls from outside the door. When you don't answer, she bangs on it. "Austy? Hey. You in there?"

The doorknob turns tentatively—but hits the invisible barrier of the lock, and stops.

"I know it's you." A rustling sound. "I see your feet under the door, you faker. I'm not going to fall for that stupid burglar routine again."A light tap on the door. "C'mon, I know you're in there."

The words fall into silence. You can feel this dark thing still bubbled up inside you, trying to burst loose.

"Austin?"

You blink. Becky always makes a point of calling you Austy, because it annoys you. Curtis is the only one allowed to call you Austy.

"If you scare me, I'm going to call Mom." Her voice quavers a little.

You look down at the razor. You're not stupid, you know it'd hurt. It'd burn sharp and clear, like digging with an icicle.

"I'm not going to scare you," you tell Becky, but it comes out sounding strange, as if your throat has rusted shut.

"Are you sick? You don't sound too good."

"I'm okay."

"Heather wants to talk to you."

"Tell her I'm busy."

You hear a couple of muffled words.

"She says to tell you it's really important."

It's like clutching at the edge of a cliff. You can give up, let go, and drop completely.

Or you can keep hanging on.

You unlock the door. You can't manage to lift your head enough to see Becky's face, but you can feel the long, startled look she's giving you.

"Here he is," she whispers into the phone, and holds it out. You take it from her, shut the door, and lock it again. The phone now hangs in your hand.

"Austin?" Heather's voice is thin and tinny, but you can hear every word. "Don't hang up."

You look at the phone. You look at it the way you look back toward land as the current pulls you slowly out to sea.

"I'm so sorry," you hear her say. "Can you hear me?"

You bring the phone to your mouth. "Yeah," you say, and now all you have to do is listen.

It's all about control, Heather says. It's all about knowing exactly what's going to happen to her, and when, and where. It's all about having a plan. And knowing the future. And not handing her life over to somebody else.

She's never trusted anybody before, she says. You're the only guy who's ever really liked her as a person. She knows that because you've always followed her rules, never pushed her to do something she doesn't want to do, and you don't tell everybody everything that happens in private. But what you did today freaked her out for a second. It was like her body put on a performance for you, while you stood there enjoying the show.

"It wasn't a show," you tell her, the first words you've said besides *yeah*. "It was just . . . us."

"I know. I know. God, I can't do this on the phone. I can't tell what you're thinking. I need to see you. I want to make everything right, Austin. Can you come over here? Please?"

You already know you're going to go. You knew it the moment you took the phone in your hand.

"Yeah," you tell Heather. And with the other hand you shut the lid of the razor's box.

CHAPTER SIXTEEN

"Are you okay?" Heather asks.

She's sitting beside you on her couch. You hadn't noticed. "Uh-huh," you answer.

She lays her head on your chest. "I can hear your heart beating," she says, nuzzling the cloth of your shirt.

She's said how sorry she is about a thousand times. And you can tell she meant it. It's not her fault that every apology fell off you like rain running down a roof. Alarms are going off in the back of your mind, warning that you shouldn't have come over, no matter how sorry she is. But the rest of you is afraid not to be here. Your pride has fallen in tangles somewhere around your ankles, but the rest of you is still clutching at the edge of that cliff.

"Do you remember the time we fell asleep together on the couch? That's the only time I ever did that. I can never sleep around anybody, much less a guy."

When you don't say anything, she raises up, examines you for a moment, before leaning in to kiss you.

"I love you," she says—and seals your mouth so that you can't say anything, even if you wanted to. A light flutter of her tongue, and then she pulls back to tuck herself into your side again. And plants yet another kiss on your chest.

It all feels vaguely pleasant. Sort of like background music, the kind that will leave absolute silence behind if it is gone.

"After you left—I've never felt like that. Like I was really completely *alone*. I thought, I've got to hear his voice. I wasn't going to say anything—just hear your voice and hang up. But all the time the phone was ringing, I was so . . ."

She doesn't finish. The TV is on, but the sound is down so low all the voices are just punctuated hums.

"You're still mad, aren't you?"

"No."

"You are. You're acting like you're not even here. You hate me, don't you?"

"I don't hate you."

"I wasn't ready—I hadn't planned to do that yet. Let you do that to me, I mean." She takes a deep breath. "You can touch me right now, if you want."

It's the last thing you want to do at this moment. You

137

could almost feel sorry for her—Heather Mackenzie, scrambling to make things up to a guy who's too empty and exhausted to respond. She gutted you, and now she thinks she can sew you up with one hand while handing you her heart with the other. What she doesn't know is that you were already only half a person, before this evening even started.

When you don't move and don't say anything, Heather sits up, pushing masses of golden hair back from her face. "You know what?" Her eyes are red rimmed.

"What?" you ask after a moment.

"I want to tell you something. I don't know if it'll make any difference—I don't know if it will even make sense. But I want to try to tell you."

She waits, staring at you. "Go ahead," you tell her.

"When I was real little, my father said he would take me fishing on the lake. And I was all excited because I'd get to ride in a boat. You know how water looks from shore, all sparkly in the sun? I thought it would be so cool to go skimming along over that. But it wasn't that way at all. We had to stab worms with hooks and drown them. And when I caught a fish, it flopped around and the pointy part of the hook was poking out from one of its eyeballs. And by the time we went back to shore, I knew that the water still *looked* shining and beautiful, but underneath it was full of all these slimy fish with staring eyeballs, and half-eaten bits of worm.

"That's the way my whole life has been," Heather adds. "Everything. And it's every guy I've been out with."

She lets the words drop. They hover there, sad and angry.

"Except for you," she says.

And then she stands up.

Her face is set now, determined. She takes your hand and gives you a gentle tug, so you obediently stand up, too. She leads you down the hall and into her room, dark except for a light shining from the open door of the closet. She takes you over to the bed. Pulls you down to sit beside her.

"Okay," she says in a breathless voice—but then doesn't move. Her thigh presses along the length of yours. Her hand squeezes yours so hard it's like being caught in a claw.

"Nobody knows this," she adds, still not moving. "I've never told anybody—you'll be the only one. And then you can use it to hurt me, if you want. And we'll be even."

You don't say anything. After a moment she grows still. You feel the deep intake of her breath, before she gets up.

She walks over to the dresser. Pauses in front of the mirror—for a second you think she's going to stop and fluff her hair—but instead she opens one of the middle drawers and pulls out the wooden box with the duck on the lid. She's moved it since you found it that time.

She opens the lid and takes out the paper. Bears it to you, holding it in her palm like something made of glass.

"This is the note he wrote to my mom. Before he died." The closet light makes her skin seem like it's glowing. "You should have seen the look on my mom's face when she tore it up. She walked away before the pieces even hit the bottom of the trash can. Like that was that, end of story. She thought it was all gone—she never knew I dug out every last piece. She doesn't know I still have it. I used to lock my door and take it out and read it sometimes."

She holds the note out, not for you to touch, but to read again if you want, in the dim light:

it's better this way i know Heather will forget i hope you will forgive

"He did it after my mom told him she wanted a divorce. He was living in the garage apartment out back. Whenever I went to see him he was just mostly sitting in his armchair, staring into space. He didn't care if I was there or not."

Sort of like the way you're behaving now.

When you look up, Heather's staring sadly at the paper.

"Maybe he was tired," you offer.

"All I know is every time I went out there I asked if I could spend the night with him, and he just said not tonight, Pumpkin, maybe another time. If he answered at all."

"Maybe he was depressed."

Funny how your mouth doesn't trip over that word. Your mouth think it's just another set of syllables to say.

But your heart knows better. It starts beating shallow, fast.

Depressed.

The last time you heard that word, Becky was the one who used it. She said she was depressed because she had a pimple on her nose. But that's not what you mean when you say that word. Not at all.

"No," Heather's saying, "he was *bitter.* He hated my mom, because she made him move out. She said it was the ultimate act of revenge. And it was—that's why he waited till he heard the car in the driveway, because he wanted her to be the one to find him. He knew he couldn't manipulate her in life, so he tried to do it in death. Only it didn't work out like he planned."

"What do you mean?"

"My mom and I were just getting back from grocery shopping, and right when we pulled up in the driveway we heard this popping noise from the garage. It sounded like a firecracker. And I was just six, you know? I thought he had some firecrackers out there. So then—"

141

She touches the paper with the tips of her fingers, pressing the black-inked letters as if there's something between the lines that can't be seen, only felt. "God. This is so useless to talk about. What happened was, my mom went to see what the noise was, and it turned out he had shot himself."

It's too tremendous an effort to think of even a single word to say. You can't even manage to raise your head again and look at her; you just keep staring straight ahead through the doorway into the dark hallway, watching the walls flash day bright, then gray for a split second, then dark, then gray again, because the television is still on in the room down the hall.

You sit there, letting the bed hold you up. Heather's frowning down at the paper in her hand.

"He was so selfish. And a coward. All he had to do was stick around a stupid garage apartment in Ohio. I mean, he had a kid, and it's not like he had to climb a mountain or do something *hard*. All he had to do was stay alive." Her shoulders give the slightest of shrugs. "So now you know. I wasn't even enough to make my own father want to stick around. Hold it over my head all you want."

She gives the note one last look before she crumples it into a hard little ball. She tosses it toward the corner wastebasket; it falls about two feet short, but she's already sitting—collapsing, really—next to you.

You put an arm around her.

"I love you, Austin," she says, just like before.

Only this time she looks at you, waiting for a reply.

Of course you have to say it. You must love her—you need her more than you've ever needed anybody. You're so addicted that you'll die if she withdraws. And she just told you she loves you. Of course you have to say it back.

She sits there with those big blue eyes, bright and clear as a little girl's eyes, as a doll's eyes, waiting to hear them: three, short, one-syllable words. Three little words—how hard could it be?

"Me, too," you finally manage. Too late. She's already shriveling a little and looking away.

You shrivel a little, too. You always figured that when you finally said that to a girl you'd feel great about it. All you can feel is that Heather Mackenzie tossed you something, and you were supposed to make one of those diving midair saves. But you—Pride of the Panthers that you are—fumbled it.

"It doesn't make any difference," you hear her say.

The two of you sit there. Heather's so still that you can't even see her breathe. You feel bad for blowing it, and after a few minutes when she turns and slides her arms around your neck, you're ready to make it up to her, thinking she just wants to be held.

But what she wants is to take back control; her lips are everywhere, fierce, marking territory, and they follow her fingers as she releases each button on your shirt.

Nipping, sucking kisses as she spreads your shirt apart. And the next thing you know her hands are pushing you backward and her fingers are tugging at your belt buckle.

You are not in the mood—of course you're not, after everything that's happened. But you don't want to hear or feel any more and you don't want to think, and you sure don't want to talk; and she's determined, insistent, and after awhile the parts of you that Heather is touching begin to insist as much as Heather herself, and it's much easier just to go along and try to comfort her this way.

Except that she won't let you kiss her. And she won't let you touch her. She just wants you to do it.

So you oblige.

It's not till near the end that you look down to see tears in her eyes—and you know you should hesitate, but your body's staked out a rhythm, and as it keeps on going you hear your voice gasp an "I love you" that sounds like an apology. And her eyes shut and she digs her nails into your back and that's when she finally does kiss you, a hard and deep kiss that sets you quivering before it pushes you over the edge.

When you finish, her eyes are dry. She still won't let you touch her, just rolls out of your reach and scoops up her clothes and says she has to go to the bathroom and she'll be right back. You don't tell her that your back stings where her fingernails left marks.

What you'd really like to do now is go home and get

in your own bed and go to sleep, but that seems kind of out of the question at the moment. So you continue to lie there alone and naked on Heather's bed, and you're suddenly very, very tired.

When she comes back in the room, she's fully dressed. "I'm going to give you a test," she says cheerfully, pulling the door shut behind her. "We'll see how well you know me."

The springs creak as she comes to sit beside you on the bed. She shuts her eyes.

"Don't look—what color are my eyes?"

"Blue," you tell her without much interest. Something's not quite right; you missed a moment somewhere back down the line and now everything seems a little off, a little skewed.

"Really blue, or do you think I wear contacts?"

"I think they're really blue."

"That's right." She opens her eyes, gives you a smile. "Contacts won't give you this color—you're either born with it, or you're not. And don't think I'm being conceited, because I'm not," she adds. "It's just the truth."

The crumpled note lies on the floor where she dropped it. She gets up, walks over to the note, picks it up, smooths it out. Puts it back in the wooden box. Places the lid on the box, and the box back in the drawer.

As she shuts the drawer, she glances at you. "You're okay now, aren't you? Everything's okay again?"

Your problem is that you dwell on things nobody else would care about. You can't seem to filter out all the silly things nobody else even notices. What's one little missed moment, when the most beautiful girl in town can't get along without you?

So you make yourself agree, from the depths of the bed. "Yes," you say, as if saying it will make it true. "Everything's perfect."

CHAPTER SEVENTEEN

Late the next afternoon you enter the field house with fingers that feel like they've gone numb, like you're going to be playing with blocks of wood, not hands, tonight. You've become disconnected from your own body, you feel like you're slipping away, even though you know you're right there in plain sight.

You crept home from Heather's house between two and three in the morning. You must have spent hours holding her and listening to her talk and talk, mostly about nothing. All you can remember now is one sentence: her voice, low and muffled, claiming that staying alive isn't hard.

That's where you screwed up; that's when you should have stopped her. You should have told her that you, Austin Reid, can understand why her father didn't stick around, and that it didn't have anything to do with her. If

147

he was like you, he was just tired of fighting. He was trying to erase a heaviness he couldn't get out from under.

In the field house you pass right by Brett Stargill, who stands in front of his locker with his back to you. You've known Brett since sixth grade, and you're close enough to toss out a hi or give him a friendly shove—but as you pass by you have the feeling that you're not real anymore. That Brett wouldn't hear you, if you did speak. That your arm would go right through if you reached to touch him.

So you don't say a word. Just go to your locker and start getting ready.

You don't talk to anybody; you perform a solitary routine of getting dressed, tucking pads into pockets and snapping them into place as if you're building the first wide receiver in the history of the world, and doing it from scratch. The routine is all that's left to glue you to this game. The Pride of the Panthers has obligations to fulfill; everyone's counting on that guy from the newspaper clipping.

The Panthers are up 14–13 with 49 seconds remaining. You personally pull in a first down at the nine, which gives the team three more shots at glory before the kicker will have to be called to put the icing on the cake.

On first-and-goal, Cox is supposed to hand off to Stargill. You take off from the line. Wheaton's cornerback goes with you, like he's supposed to. You cut inside, and when you glance back to check the progress of the play, Stargill's slipped or tripped or something—he's on one knee in the backfield, just getting up—the play is busted and Cox is looking for an open receiver. As arms wrap him up, Cox's head swivels back and forth; he's searching, for someone—for anyone.

You've already slowed, yelled to him, and as he goes down his eyes click on you, and then his pass—more of a toss, really—is lofting your way.

At that moment you feel Wheaton's cornerback breathing down your neck—but your hands are open and the ball is sailing toward you and it's going to hit you right on the numbers. You're ready, ready to run.

Too ready.

You turn, trying to tuck in the ball a split second too soon, and somehow it pops off your hands. It seems to hover for a second, wobbling on your fingertips.

You're right on the goal line; this should be a done deal. But Wheaton's cornerback gets a hand up between you and that wobbling ball.

And that's all it takes—he's off, cradling the football like it's a baby.

Blame comes down in one loud groan from the crowd. You're in what feels like a nightmare of slow motion; an all-out lunge at his back turns into a grab at his legs, which turns out to be a clutch at the air where his

149

ankle used to be. And you're left behind, face down on the turf while Wheaton's cornerback takes the ball back almost to the Parkersville twenty before somebody manages to drive him out of bounds.

Three downs later, with just eighteen seconds left on the clock, their kicker clears a field goal. The game ends at 16–14, Wheaton.

This loss is a personal gift from you.

Some mistakes you have a choice about. You can ease out from under them by apologizing—or changing your ways. Or just deciding not to think about them anymore.

But certain kinds of mistakes are carved in stone. No matter what you do, no matter whether you think about them or not.

Back at the field house after the game, you shower and change and go out to meet Heather. You stand on the concrete square just outside the field house door, hands jammed in your pockets, looking around the parking lot for her.

She's not there.

Now that you think about it, she might have said something about going somewhere this weekend. Now you wish you had at least made the effort to listen, when she was doing all that talking last night.

You wait awhile longer, just in case, watching the parking lot clear out, and when you have no reason to wait anymore, you step onto the asphalt alone.

At home, you walk into your room and that guy is still clinging to the bulletin board as if nothing's happened. Grinning his blank grin.

You pull out the tack that holds him to the cork and take the clipping into the bathroom, where you tear him into tiny pieces. You flush them and watch the little flakes circle before they disappear.

It's still dark outside when you open your eyes. Becky's not up yet, or Mom. It's awfully quiet in the house, without all those bustling noises you usually hear at the edges of your sleep.

You look at the clock: four-thirty. It's Sunday morning.

The alarm is set for eight. Three and a half more hours.

You don't want to go to church today. It feels strange to admit that—you don't want to sit with bowed head while all those dreary words rain guilt on you. You've stepped out into empty space this weekend; you've been hanging in that one endless moment before you fall, and you cannot take on even one more syllable of weight.

So after a long while, you reach over to turn off the alarm. As of 4:53 A.M. you are officially not going to church today, no matter what anybody says.

The only thing in this world that seems even halfway solid is Heather, and the only thing that interests you in the slightest is hearing her voice.

Around midmorning, while Mom and Becky are gone, you try to call.

Mrs. Mackenzie answers. "Austin, is that you? Hi, honey. No, she's spending the weekend in Fort Worth and won't be back till tonight. You know Lacy Matthews, don't you?" She adds a bunch of stuff explaining the hows and whys of Heather being in Fort Worth, but none of it makes sense till she adds, "She'll be back tonight, though. I'll tell her to give you a call if it's not too late. How's that?"

"Fine," you tell her. Although it's not, really.

All you can do after that is go back to bed, pull the pillow over your head, and wait for the phone to ring.

Noises work their way into what's left of your sleep; clanks and chings and the sound of a running tap.

Before your eyes even open, the burden descends: It's Monday, and Heather never called. You've pretty much been in bed for the last twenty-four hours. You told Mom you didn't feel well, which was about as close as you could come to describing the way you really do feel.

The sounds keep on incessantly; dishes and silverware and the splash of water—until they finally add up and you remember. When the dishwasher broke a couple of days ago Mom asked you to please be the official dishwasher till she could get the real one fixed.

Only you kept forgetting. Then all day yesterday, you didn't so much as lift a finger. And now Mom might be late for work.

So you force yourself to get up. When you walk into the kitchen, Mom's standing at the sink, an apron over her work clothes. She glances over her shoulder when she hears you but turns back to the sink and doesn't say anything.

That's Mom; she could have nagged you or left a note, but she just let the dishes pile up, assuming you'd eventually do as you promised—until it got to where she could barely get to the faucet to fill a pot of water for coffee.

Now she stands here with her back to you, washing the dishes that you should have already taken care of.

You head for the sink, hold out your hand for the scrubber. "I'll do that."

"No, I will. I want to make sure it gets done."

"Come on, Mom. I'll do it."

"I've already gotten started." She keeps washing.

Okay, you'll dry for her, then. You're better at it than she is, anyway. She just sort of swipes at them, then sticks them in the cabinets.

You open the drawer for a dish towel. "Sorry I forgot," you tell her, picking up a glass and getting to work.

Mom gives one last extra-hard scrub to the pan she's

working on and then relents. "It's all right. I'm glad to see you're feeling better today." She shakes her head. "Hard to believe you used to *beg* me to let you wash dishes."

"That was years ago, Mom. Maybe first grade."

"That long?" Mom frowns, sets the pan on the drainboard. She pauses, watching the way you dry the inside of the glass; since your hands are too big to fit, you have to wad the towel up and shove it down inside. "Next thing you're going to tell me is that seven-pound, six-ounce baby boy I gave birth to is already taller than I am." She smiles. "You were always a good little dryer. You'd be standing there biting your lip, working so hard. Always took things like that so seriously, for such a little kid."

You set the glass to the side and pick up a brass-bottomed pan, thinking how strange it is to hear her talk like this. Mom's never been one for reminiscing. Every other family you know has photo albums; your mom's never even bought a camera.

So hearing this sort of thing is like salve on a raw wound. "That's the first time in a long time I've heard you say anything about when I was little," you tell her. "Or Becky, either. You don't talk about it much."

Mom starts scrubbing again. "No, I guess I don't. They weren't great times. Your father getting sick and all, and then he was gone. And me with a toddler and a newborn, and the horses weren't bringing in any money. Lord, it broke my heart to sell my horses." She sighs.

"Sometimes you can't look back if you want to keep moving forward. I had to keep moving forward, Austin. Still do."

"But you remember things about me and Becky."

"Of course. Didn't I just say you were a good little dryer?"

You give the brass-bottomed pan a final polish and pick up a wet saucepan. "What other things do you remember?"

"Well. Let's see. You were my helper. I never had to worry about you. Becky was the one I had to keep an eye on. Like the time she cut her own hair with the nail scissors."

"I remember that. It looked like she went after it with a weed eater."

"I always hid the nail scissors after that. But you were a different story." Mom's smiling to herself again. "Do you remember the time you decided you were going to help me by folding the laundry?"

You shake your head no, put down the saucepan, pick up a large glass bowl, wiping it carefully.

"I guess you were about three. It was one of those bad, busy times; I was pregnant with Becky and your dad was in the hospital. Nothing was getting done around the house; the whole place was a disaster. And there was a big old basket of clean clothes in the utility room that needed to be ironed. But you didn't know it still had to be ironed;

you thought you'd just up and take care of it yourself. Of course, you were just a little guy, littler than the clothes you were trying to fold. So I found you sitting back there in the middle of this big old stack of clothes, wrestling with one of my blouses, frustrated as all get-out. You weren't making a sound, just working away with little bitty tears rolling down your cheeks. I put the blouse in my drawer all wrinkled in a wad," she adds, her smile twisting, "'cause I couldn't stand to tell you it wasn't right. You've always been a good kid, Austin. I guess I don't tell you that often enough."

The bowl is dry. You set it down, start in on a skillet.

"Time moves so fast," she says quietly. "You blink and suddenly your kids are almost grown up." She sighs and starts washing again.

She's on the last pan. It's quiet in the kitchen now, except for Mom's swishing and scrubbing.

You want to hang on to this moment. Just a bit longer, anyway. "I remember how Dad used to let me shave," you tell her.

She gives you a funny look. "Shave?"

"I mean, like, play shaving. You know, how Dad used to set me on the counter while he shaved? He used to put shaving cream on my face and let me shave with a toy razor."

"I don't think you ever had a toy razor."

"I did. I remember it. It must have gotten lost. I even

remember shaving in the bathtub, with bubbles from the bubble bath—only I had to use a comb turned around backward, for the razor. I remember it wasn't the same as when Dad helped me."

"I really don't think it was Daddy. He was pretty sick, hon. He didn't even have any hair because of the chemo, and by the time they stopped that, he couldn't shave himself, much less you." She rinses the pan. "I'll bet it was Curtis's dad you remember. You spent a lot of time over there when Daddy was in the hospital."

It *was* Daddy, you think. You realize you've been drying the same skillet for a while now. It's bone dry.

"Are you still using that fancy razor of his?" Mom asks.

You nod, and set the skillet down.

"Better than gathering dust in a cabinet. I'm glad you found it and brought it out. This may sound silly," she adds, "but it makes me feel like you'll get to make good use of all the chances he never had." She glances at you. "You've got circles under your eyes. You sure you feel up to school today?" She takes the towel out of your hand. "I can finish this. You don't have to be up for another hour or so—why don't you go back to bed, see if you can get a bit more sleep?"

You *don't* need more sleep. No, you feel fine. And you're not going back to bed. Instead, you head straight for the bathroom. Lock the door behind you.

It was not Mr. Hightower. It was your father.

Run the hot water while you take off your T-shirt. Open the cabinet and take out the shaving gel, the razor. Pull the hand towel off the rack and lay it neatly beside the sink. Wait for the water to get hot.

Your crystal-clear memory is not cheap. Or washed out. Or somebody else's.

After a few minutes you check the water with one finger. It's ready. You wipe your finger on the hand towel and fill the sink. When it's about to run over, you shut the faucet off, and dive into the ritual of shaving.

Yep. You've always liked being the unfrayed end of a tradition that's been passed from father to son all down the generations. Starting with a straight-edged razor and a leather strap.

You're turning your head this way and that, measuring the path of metal over skin. The razor feels light, like your dad's hand swiping the foam onto your cheeks. In your mind, you're sitting on the counter, feet dangling off until your dad lifts you down, and your feet landing solid on the blue tile floor. You remember that blue tile, cool under your bare feet.

Blue tile.

But the floor under your feet is white.

The truth wrings you out slowly, like a sponge.

This, the only bathroom in your house, is white— white tile, white paint, white everything. It always has been.

The Hightowers' bathroom has blue tile on the floor, reaching halfway up the wall to cream-and-blue patterned wallpaper. The wallpaper's changed over the years, but the tile has been blue ever since you can remember.

And you used to be this pitiful, hopeful kid hanging around the Hightowers' house, trying to soak up any father-son atmosphere left over from Curtis and his dad.

Don't look at the mirror anymore. That guy saws at you, he's going to cut you completely loose.

Be a machine. Clean off the razor. Place it back in its box. Wipe any traces of foam from your cheeks and neck.

Standing there holding the towel, you notice how the tendons are bunched lines along your forearm; how the blood rushes through the veins in your wrist. You can almost hear it, whispering along the blue-walled tunnels.

No.

Put one foot in front of the other, all the way to the phone. Take it back into the bathroom, where you are insulated from the rest of the household, where the razor is still sitting there in its box by the sink.

Your fingers are hitting the buttons on the phone, in the correct order, all on their own. You don't even need to look at the numbers. When Heather answers sleepily, you speak almost in a whisper, because these words are for no one but Heather. "Let's ditch school today," you tell her. "Let's just take the day off and go somewhere."

"Austin?" She sounds groggy.

"Yeah, it's me."

"What time is it?"

"I don't know."

"It's . . . five till six. God. What are you asking me?"

"To let me pick you up so we can—"

"Is something wrong?"

Silence. It's a very simple question.

"Hello?" She sounds irritated. "Are you there?"

"Yeah."

"You called and woke me up. Is something wrong?"

Did you ever have this feeling like you're not sad or anything, but like something's squeezing the back of your eyes? "No," you hear yourself tell her. "Nothing's wrong. I just missed you this weekend."

"God. Why is it you early risers always assume everybody else is up, just because you are? It's not even light out." She sighs, and you hear the rustle of bedclothes. "Okay, let me get this straight. You called me at five till six to ask me not to go to school today just because you missed me? I mean, I'm glad you missed me, but couldn't it wait?"

The wooden box sits there, unmoving. The lid is shut so you can't see the razor, but you know it's there. It's metal, that's all. Just metal. A tool. Cold when left in its box, warm when it's been held awhile.

There's no hurry. You can hang on till you see her, can't you? All you have to do is nothing, until you can see

Heather and dig even just one finger back into solid ground.

Deep breath. "Yeah," you tell her. "It can wait."

"Great. I'm touched, I really am, but I can't ditch school for you. Not today. You know my schedule, right? So you can catch me between classes. And I'll meet you after practice. Okay?"

"Yeah," you tell her again. What else can you say?

After hanging up, you don't put the box back in the cabinet, but leave it by the sink. Don't take a shower, either, just go to your room to throw on some clothes.

When you leave, the razor is still there in its place, waiting to see what's going to happen when you come home.

CHAPTER EIGHTEEN **18**

You see Heather for a brief moment between classes and try to walk with her, but her friends are there and she's laughing and gossiping with them, pulling you down the hall beside her, with one hand latched onto your arm. It's not what you need from her; whatever it is that you need will have to wait till afternoon.

The day inches by.

After school, when you're heading across the parking lot to the field house, football is just a long, dark tunnel that you can't escape.

When you walk into the field house, Coach isn't there. There's a note on the marker board, written in broad, square black letters:

SUIT UP AND GO TO THE FIELD.

And, below that:

FULL PADS.

On the field, Coach is standing on the grass alone, apart from the gathering players. He's got both hands in his jacket pockets and he's staring toward the scarred goalpost as he lets one of the assistants put the team through warm-ups.

He doesn't acknowledge you when you walk past. When warm-ups are over and he finally turns around, he does just what you expected. He gives you one glance then spits in the dirt—Coach doesn't like having a hardened ball-bobbler on his team—and tells the other guys to get in a circle. He tells you to go stand in the middle. Just like you knew he would.

You pull on your helmet and head into the middle of all those eyes.

Coach stands a few feet outside the circle, hands in his pockets. "I got some news for you boys," he announces. "This is football. And in football, you're going to get hit. Some of y'all don't seem to be able to get that idea into your heads."

When he takes his hands out of his pockets, there's something in them. It's a long torn strip of towel. "I got a variation that's going to do you some good, Reid," he says. "This works wonders for receivers. Take your helmet off for a second."

You obey, and he walks toward you with that long cloth. "Anybody on this team wants to listen for footsteps—that's all they're gonna do, is listen."

He uses the piece of towel for a blindfold. The last thing you see before he ties it on is Curtis looking like he smells something bad, and then the thing is on so tight that the terry cloth bends your eyelashes.

All the things you do wrong, all the missed moments—and still everybody thought you were the Pride of the Panthers. It's only right that you should be the one to get pounded. It should have been you all along.

You fumble your helmet back into place and stand, waiting. You hear how all the other guys are dead quiet, hear how birds are squawking in a tree across the track. You can hear your heart beating thinly inside your chest.

And then something else—a faint snapping sound, followed by a hollow thud on the grass near your feet.

"Hightower?" That's Coach.

But you don't hear Curtis answer.

"Hightower," Coach grunts, a little louder.

No sound from Curtis.

And then you hear Coach say grimly, "Whatever. Let's get to work."

He blows the whistle.

You hear pads creak; you even think you can hear cleats gripping grass, in the moment before something smashes into you and then the ground slams up to crush what's left of your breath from your lungs.

Suck more air in. Struggle to your feet.

The whistle blows again.

Coach must be taking it easy since you can't see. It's the first time all season he hasn't called them on two at a time. And he gives you enough time to get up, in between.

Eventually you're lying there and no more whistles sound and you hear Coach say, "All right. Looks like we could use some sled practice. Get moving, ladies."

Your tailbone is hurting, and the back of your skull where it meets your backbone. But you get up, and, like Curtis, you don't complain.

When you remove your helmet and reach up to fumble at the knotted towel, Coach's fingers are there, untying it for you. "You're a good player, son," he's saying quietly. "Don't let your imagination keep you from being a great one."

When the knot comes loose and the blindfold disappears back into Coach's pocket, you immediately look around for Curtis.

He's not there. Not heading out toward the sleds with everybody else. Not running laps, like he should be if Coach is mad at him. He's not anywhere that you can see.

"Go get some water and hightail it back out here." Coach's face is set in tired lines as he turns away. "Dobie," you hear him say. "Get that thing out of my sight."

That's when you see the lone empty helmet lying on the grass.

Dobie lopes over to it. Coach is already bellowing at

somebody else. "Baker!" he calls. "This ain't bumper cars—wrap 'em up, you hear?"

Dobie bends, loops his long fingers through Curtis's face mask. You watch as he slowly takes the helmet off the field.

Nobody you know has ever just walked out of football practice. Failed to show up, yes. Pretended to be sick, yes. Back in ninth grade, Dobie even went to the counselor and got his schedule changed to regular PE. But nobody's ever just walked out, right in the middle of a drill.

Leave it to Curtis to decide he didn't like the view from this particular tunnel.

Heather shows up right before the end. The sight of her doesn't lift you up the way you thought it would.

You wave at her, anyway, and try to smile.

Later, when you come out of the field house clean and dressed in street clothes, Curtis's car is nowhere to be seen. Dobie stands on the sidewalk, shading his eyes, looking around the parking lot.

Poor forgotten Dobie. Stranded here because of you and Curtis. "Need a ride home?" you ask.

Dobie peers at your pickup. Heather's visible inside it; she's probably running down the battery by listening to the radio. "You sure it's okay?"

"It's okay."

"Well. All right. 'Preciate it, Austin."

The two of you walk side by side across the parking

lot. But when you're about to reach the cab, Dobie heads toward the bed of the truck.

Good old Dobie.

"Come on up front, Dobe. Heather can sit in the middle."

"It's okay. I'll ride in the back."

"There's plenty of room."

Dobie hesitates again, with a glance at the back window—at Heather's blond head. It's the same look he has when he passes the show window of the local car dealership, of longing being quickly nipped in the bud. "I'll be fine back here," he says with dignity, and puts one booted foot on the trailer hitch to hoist himself up.

"We're giving Dobie a ride home," you tell Heather as you slide in, and she stares at you for a moment before looking quickly over her shoulder.

"Oh," she says. "For a moment I thought you'd meant I was going to have to be all squished up next to him. The gods of dating are kind, after all."

"He's a nice guy," you tell her.

"Maybe so, but I'd rather walk through Kmart in sponge rollers than have to rub against him around every corner." She glances at Dobie in the rearview mirror, then gives you a smile. "This way, he can dip tobacco if he wants, and I can be alone with you, and we're all happy. You are going to take him home first, aren't you?"

That means a trip out 171 and back, but you nod anyway.

You let Dobie off at the road in front of his house like you always have. You don't get to say good-bye because he doesn't come up to the window—he never does—just thumps on the fender like he's dismissing a horse with a pat on the flank. Then he goes to check the mailbox before heading up the dirt driveway to his family's small frame house.

All the way back to her house Heather's talking to you, fooling with the radio. She doesn't say a word about your phone call this morning. When you pull up in front of her house you don't get out right away. She scoots closer and nestles against you, talking on and on about how in sixth period Mrs. Henderson hates her and is desperate for a chance to flunk her.

All the while she's talking, she's also playing with your right hand, testing its size against hers, tracing the outlines of your fingers.

So finally you give your full attention to Heather, bright and beautiful and curled up against you, and you understand that in order to make this connection you are going to have to put yourself on the line.

"I wasn't even enough to make my own father want to stick around," she said. You've got the missing pieces to her puzzle—you can start by pointing out that she's been looking at her dad with tunnel vision. That she doesn't see the whole picture. That she can't take other people's suicides so personally. And if she asks how you know, well . . .

"I've been thinking," you begin. Only when she stops talking do you realize you interrupted her, but now you've got the momentum and you're not going to stop. "About your father," you add.

You can't tell any reaction. She's fingering the design on your class ring.

"I've been thinking," you repeat carefully, "that your mom could be wrong about that manipulation stuff. Because it could be that he just didn't want to lie there for a long time without being found. Maybe that's why he did it right when your mom was pulling up. So it might not have had anything to do with revenge."

Heather is silent, leaning against you. "I really don't want to talk about this," she finally says.

"I know. But just listen for a second. You said he was bitter. I was thinking that maybe he just didn't see any point in being alive anymore."

"No point." Her voice is muffled against your shirt. "Just me."

"He probably felt pretty low, pretty unimportant. Like everybody would get over it real quick."

Heather sits up and moves away a little. "Is this why you woke me up this morning? Well, you can just drop it. You don't even know what you're talking about. He was selfish," she adds, her mouth a tight line. "And a liar."

"A liar? What did he lie about?"

"Everything. Calling me Pumpkin. The hugs. The

kisses. Everything."

"I don't think he was lying. I think he cared about you a lot. And selfish—well, maybe he was. But maybe he couldn't help it. It could be that he didn't really want to die, he just wanted to stop feeling bad. But he couldn't see any other way—"

"Why are you even bringing this up? You don't know anything about it. You have no clue."

No clue? Just a razor waiting for you at home.

"But I do," you tell her. "Kind of."

"No, you don't."

"Maybe not in some ways, but there's still some things I see that—"

"Oh, of *course* you see. You were there, right?"

"No, but—"

"I was. I was there. Hello?—and *you* weren't!"

"But—"

"It wasn't my mom who found him, Austin."

It takes a moment for her words to sink in, for you to catch her meaning. "Oh," you hear yourself say, and for a moment you sound like that guy from the mirror, being squeezed.

"You have no clue," Heather says again, through gritted teeth. "Well, here's a clue. Here's *several* clues. He was lying there in his armchair, all laid back with the footrest out. There was this smell, like—when people die," she says, enunciating each word carefully. "Austin, when people die, they lose control of everything. Like, their bowels? And the blood—I'll bet you didn't even know blood has a smell. Well it does, when there's a lot of it. A thick, heavy smell. It was all over everything—the chair, the floor, the wall. And clumps of . . . his head. My father's head. So don't even *think* you know anything about it."

In a flash the world shifts and you see yourself from some weird, outside angle where dying is not some healing, endless sleep; where it is not the relief you've always thought it would be—like opening a spillway eases the pressure off a dam.

It is an action that will fly completely out of your control.

It is a man sprawled in his own shit and blood.

Here in the truck, it's very quiet. Heather clears her throat and looks away; you realize you've been staring at her. Now you see how pale she is.

"You're right, I don't know anything about that," you tell her quietly. "But I think I know something about *why* he did it. And—I think I can help you see that it's not what you think. That it wasn't anything against you. Because . . ."

You can feel your left hand tightening, squeezing the steering wheel, trying to crush it into dust. "Because I know how he felt. Your dad. Sort of. Because, I guess I tend to, you know, sometimes . . . feel the same way."

Heather's voice is high, pinched. "What do you mean? Feel what way?"

"Down, I guess. I don't know the best word for it. Maybe . . . depressed. Like . . . not being . . ."

Your heart's thumping so loud, she must be able to hear it.

"Sometimes I want to kill myself."

There it is. Out on the table. The steering wheel is still there, uncrushed, and your left hand is still on it, and you can still feel it.

And you can feel Heather staring at you.

"So," you say carefully, giving her silence a light prod. "I guess you think I'm a little weird, huh?"

She doesn't answer. You sneak a glance at her; she looks a little shocked. And this time you know the exact missed moment, right as it happens. It happens when she says: "Don't touch me."

Sure enough, she's right—your hand was reaching toward hers. You didn't even know it. You pull it back to the seat by your side.

"And don't look at me like you expect something. Don't act like *you're* surprised at *me*. *You* are the one who is not *normal*."

She looks away from you and starts collecting her stuff to leave.

"I can't believe this," you hear her muttering as she bends over to feel for her purse and books. "It's like, do I *attract* suicidal people?" She gets her hands on her books, which have spread out on the floorboard, and starts piling them back into one stack. "Or did you start out regular and something about me makes you want to blow your brains out?" She sits up, not looking at you as she pulls her books into her lap, hauls her purse up by the tangled strap. "I am not going to wallow around in your mental problems." Her eyes are straight ahead, but her hand trembles when she pulls her purse strap up onto her shoulder.

She opens the door and slides out—but instead of shutting the door, she stops. She bends to look right into your face. She's got one last grenade to lob.

"Let me make this clean and clear. Don't even think you're going to walk me to the door. And don't try to call me later. Don't try to call me ever. You are *sick*, and this is over. O-V-E-R."

She flings the words at you, looking at you from wide, frightened doll's eyes. Then, *slam!*—she's scurrying up the sidewalk.

You watch her through the window. At first she hurries as if something's chasing her, but by the time she gets to the porch steps her back is straight, her shoulders squared. In that instant you want to run after her, you want to crawl after a girl who just made a major point of not wanting you.

You keep both hands at your sides. Your head turns, your eyes follow her up onto the porch—but otherwise you don't move. You do not open your mouth. You just sit there and watch her leave.

She disappears inside; the front door shuts.

It's o-v-e-r.

You look at the window that is Heather's bedroom. The blinds are closed, but in a moment you see them give a little shudder—you can almost see her, stalking into her room, slamming the door so hard it shakes the blinds. You can almost see her at this moment, checking herself out in the mirror. Calming herself down by taking out a brush, maybe fluffing her hair. Thinking she doesn't look so bad, for someone who just got so freaked out. Telling herself there's nothing in that mirror that looks wounded or damaged.

Heather Mackenzie is completely capable of keeping everything shining and perfect around her. And she doesn't need you.

You start the engine. Put the truck in gear and drive away from her house.

The next thing you know, you're passing through the middle of town. Already? You don't remember getting here; time must have stopped keeping pace somehow. It's like driving through a doll's town, with little wooden people walking on the streets—this town seems to have been deserted of real people years ago. All the cars moving like robots, the changing of lights from red to green to yellow—it all seems hollow, like a not very good copy of real life.

It isn't until you're forced to stop for a red light on 171 that you finally see another real live human being. An old guy, wrinkled and windblown in a thin jacket. He's on the median, selling Tyler roses.

You've got some money in your pocket. You could buy flowers, drive back. Surprise Heather with some roses.

You could act like there's nothing wrong with you at all. Act like there's nothing wrong with her, either. See if you can get back on the same road the two of you were on before this weekend.

The old guy's got a thin bundle in his hand; in the unreal glow of the dying daylight you see red roses wrapped in clear cellophane. You could pay him a few bucks, take the roses and lay them carefully on the seat beside you so they wouldn't get bent. You could make a U-turn, nice and easy so the roses wouldn't slide off onto the floorboard. You could drive slow and careful back to Heather's house and try to make everything all right.

You take another look at the roses. They're just buds, actually. Tied up with a cheap, shiny ribbon already unraveled a little on one end.

Heather wouldn't like flowers from some guy off the street. She's probably used to florist flowers, done up in a vase with a card, delivered by a van with lettering on the side.

Of course, she might not be able to tell where they came from.

But you have a feeling that she would.

The light is already green. There's nobody behind you telling you to move on. Or even to turn back.

You ease off on the clutch at the same moment you slowly begin to press the accelerator. And in a moment you're heading down the highway toward home.

CHAPTER NINETEEN

When you finally get home, you pull up the gravel driveway past the house, and head around to the back. You park in your usual spot by the back porch and cut the engine.

There is only one thing left.

You sit perfectly still and you shut your eyes, and listen to yourself breathe.

The truck seat is firm under you. The air is cool; it hugs your shirt to your skin. It's peaceful in here. It's like being on the bottom of a pool, in the stillness and the silence, while up above you the ripples are still spreading.

In the quiet a sound begins; a sound that you can't identify; rhythmic, muffled through the window.

You open the door, and the noise gets louder. It is coming from across the front yard. From the Hightowers' house? It's harsher now, regular—almost a scratching sound.

It must be Curtis. Nobody else would be over there at this time of day.

Curtis will be pretty torn up when he finds out you're gone. Maybe you ought to go over, give him one last moment. A good-bye, whether he knows it or not. Something, because you owe him, for what you're about to do.

Although the truth is, talking to Curtis isn't going to make any of this easier for him. Probably you should just go inside. It's going to be getting dark soon. You should walk inside and go stand in front of the sink and let that razor blade do its job. Sure, some people are going to be hurt. Curtis. Mom. Becky. But eventually they'll heal. They'll all get over it, with time.

Of course, Heather's dad probably thought the same thing.

The thought ruffles your sense of peace. You try to smooth it back down, try to breathe deep and recapture the silence of a moment ago, but that sound from outside is scraping the air around you. So you sit there for you don't know how long, breathing too fast, staring at what's left of the vine-covered old fence that lies along the property line between your house and Curtis's; a few weathered old posts in varying degrees of decay and uprightness, held in their positions by a couple of rusted coils of wire, the whole thing covered with blackberry vines.

You and Curtis used to set empty cans on those posts,

throwing rocks at them for target practice. That was a long time ago, but now you're remembering how, when all the cans were knocked off, you and Curtis would walk over to reset them and end up taking a break every time, filling up with blackberries, talking and laughing about nothing in particular while the afternoon shadows grew longer and longer.

You and Curtis always tried to stretch the days out, because no day was ever long enough, back then.

You get out of the cab. Everything had stopped, inside your truck—but now that you're out, you've got to make choices.

Choices, it seems, have fingers reaching out in every direction. To the future. And the past.

That's why you follow the sound over to the Hightowers' house. And find Curtis scraping paint off the front porch railing as if this is a day like any other.

"Hey," he greets you, not pausing in his scraping.

"Hey." Then, "Getting ready to paint?"

Stupid question. Curtis, of course, doesn't bother to answer.

You walk over, sit on the front steps. These are the same steps you and Curtis used to leap off when you were little, seeing who could jump the farthest. Only problem was, neither of you ever marked where you landed, so neither ever knew who won.

The scraping stops. Curtis brushes paint flakes away,

smoothing the wood with his hand. After a few more moments you remember today's football practice.

"Where'd you go?" you ask him.

Curtis just shrugs.

You already know, anyway. He didn't want to be there anymore—so he undid his chin strap, dropped his helmet on the ground, and walked away.

Now, sitting here, you realize something else, because of Curtis and his dad; because Curtis has never gone to visit his father in the whole five years since his dad left. Never called him, even. And he never will.

When you think about that, you understand that Curtis made a decision when he walked off the field this afternoon. He'll never go back—not to sit on the bench, not to play, not even to watch a game from the stands. That's the way Curtis is. For him, this football season is over.

All because of you.

Curtis is scraping again, pressing the razor's edge along the wood in rhythmic strokes.

"I'm sorry, man," you tell him.

"Why?"

"If I'd been able to hold on to the ball—"

"Forget it. Couldn't stand one more second of that beer-bellied Nazi asshole."

"Yeah, but if—"

"Doesn't matter. Whole thing gave me a bad taste in

my mouth." He frowns a little, then scrapes harder.

A large flake of paint has landed on your knee. You pick it up and break it in half. Then you break it in half again. And again. Finally, when it's so small it's disappeared on the end of your finger, you clear your throat. "Heather and I broke up," you tell Curtis.

The thought of what that means—aimless hours, nobody to get out of bed for, nobody who can make you real—leaves one big unshed ache in your chest.

"You okay?" Curtis is asking.

You start to shrug, but your eyes sting with sudden tears and somehow you're shaking your head no.

Curtis rasps steadily away at the railing. Just when you think he's not going to comment, he says, "I know. Hurts like hell."

You're remembering how you wanted to leave, that morning in the tack room long ago, but didn't. Curtis won't leave either—whatever you choose to tell him.

"Actually," you hear yourself say, "I've been kind of thinking about killing myself lately."

The scraping stops.

"How?" Curtis asks, after a moment, and even though you can hear a little worry hovering at the edge of that one-word question, for one crazy split second you actually think you might laugh.

Anybody else would have asked *why*.

You should have known Curtis is too practical for

that. Curtis always starts at the outside of a problem and works his way in—like peeling an onion.

Sitting there in his presence, a bare possibility stirs; the possibility that letting go of the cliff's edge may not mean that you have to fall.

The words are more than ready. They rise up through the catch in your throat and tumble out into raw, jumbled piles: Heather and her father; heaviness, football, and razors. After a few minutes, Curtis quits pretending to scrape paint; he comes around with the scraper still in his hand and sits beside you on the steps.

And you sit there talking: Curtis, flicking the button on the scraper, clicking the razor in, then out, then in again, thinking hard, interrupting with a question once in a while; you, picking up flakes of paint, splitting them smaller and smaller, feeling your way into the future that you hadn't been able to see.

Millions of people suffer from depression or know someone who does. If you want to know more about depression and what you can do to get help, contact the following organizations for information:

American Academy of Child and Adolescent Psychiatry (AACAP)
3615 Wisconsin Avenue, NW
Washington, DC 20016-3007
(202) 966-7300
(800) 333-7636
www.aacap.org

American Psychiatric Association
1400 K Street, NW
Washington, DC 20005
(888) 357-7924
www.psych.org

American Psychological Association
750 First Street, NE
Washington, DC 20002-4242
(202) 336-5500
(800) 374-2721
www.apa.org/psychnet

Center for Mental Health Services–Knowledge Exchange Network
(KEN)
P.O. Box 42490
Washington, DC 20015
(800) 789-2647
www.mentalhealth.org

National Institute of Mental Health
NIMH Public Inquiries
6001 Executive Boulevard, Rm 8184, MSC 9663
Bethesda, MD 20892-9663
(301) 443-4513
www.nimh.nih.gov

If you or someone you know is having suicidal thoughts, seek help immediately. The following hotlines are answered twenty-four hours a day, seven days a week:

National Hope Line Network: (800) 784-2433
Girls and Boys Town National Hotline: (800) 448-3000